The Line Rider

With his job as a line rider under threat, Mack Cambray hopes to settle down with his bride as a homesteader. However, in trying to solve the mystery of his wife's untimely death, Mack ends up in the middle of a violent range war.

The Line Rider

K.S. Stanley

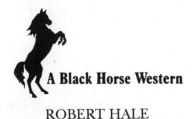

A Black Horse Western

ROBERT HALE

© K.S. Stanley 2018
First published in Great Britain 2018

ISBN 978-0-7198-2809-6

The Crowood Press
The Stable Block
Crowood Lane
Ramsbury
Marlborough
Wiltshire SN8 2HR

www.bhwesterns.com

Robert Hale is an imprint
of The Crowood Press

Typeset by
Derek Doyle & Associates, Shaw Heath
Printed and bound in Great Britain by
4Bind Ltd, Stevenage, SG1 2XT

PROLOGUE

The crowd fell silent as the salesman walked up onto a small platform behind the fence at the far end of the corral. 'I wish to thank you all for coming here today!' he shouted out, 'You are about to see a spectacle, the like of which most of you will have never seen before, and which I guarantee will take your breath away! I also wish to thank a group of your local cattlemen, without whom what you are about to see would not have been possible! They have rounded up a small herd of the most aggressive longhorns they could find and, in a moment, will drive them into this corral!' The crowd gasped and some people started to retreat from the perimeter of the corral. 'I maintain that these ferocious beasts will be tamed by this corral's special fencing and no one will come to any harm!'

'The man's mad, Judd,' Holden Bauldry cried out as the two men stood watching the proceedings below from the first-floor balcony of Miss Kittie's boarding house.

'Yer don't think that wire fence is gonna stop those long-horns, do yer?' Judd Rames asked his colleague. 'I've heard some say this new wire is very effective and much better than smooth wire.'

'Yeah, but they're all drunks or attention seekers!' Holden spat the words out angrily. As the thunderous sound of charging cattle hoofs filled the air, Bauldry raised his Winchester rifle and looked down the length of the barrel. He figured that if he took out the first longhorn several yards before it reached the end of the corral, the others would fall over its body.

'Drop the rifle, mister!' Holden felt the cold barrel of a six-shooter being pressed into his neck. He heard its hammer being pulled back. 'Don't you move either, mister,' the gun's owner said to Judd Rames, pointing a second revolver in his direction. It was Miss Kittie.

'Now, put that rifle down slowly,' she said confidently, 'an' no harm will come to you or your friend here and to no one in the crowd below.'

'But ma'am. . . .' Holden protested as he did what he was told cautiously.

'Ain't no buts, mister,' Miss Kittie replied, kicking the Winchester away from Bauldry. 'Jest trust me an' be amazed at what you are about to see.'

Holden peered over balcony as the ferocious longhorns were let loose into the corral. Offended by the constraints the corral imposed on their freedom, they charged at the barbed wire fence, kicking up a cloud of dust. To the amazement of the crowd the longhorns backed away, as the sharp barbs on the fence wire dug into their hide. Surprised yet not deterred, the cattle regrouped and charged again but with the same end result: another victory to the barbs. Then, no longer prepared to endure any more pain, the cattle surrendered and stood quietly in the corral as the crowd cheered.

'You knew that was gonna happen, didn't yer?' Holden said, looking angrily at the woman who had pulled a gun on him.

'Yes, I did, but I didn't wanna spoil yer fun,' Miss Kittie replied. 'I saw the original demonstration back in '76, about eighteen months ago over in San Antonio, given by someone else, John W Gates to be precise. This guy's jest a copycat. I am sure his wire is good but I suspect he's a moonshiner.'

'Moonshiner?' Judd queried.

'Yep,' Miss Kittie confirmed. 'He's probably copyin' someone else's design an' not payin' royalties so he can sell his wire cheaper.'

'You seem to know a lot about this,' Holden remarked.

'A lot of people who pass through here and stay in this guest house are in the barbed wire business,' Miss Kittie explained. 'Some folk who ain't refer to barbed wire as the devil's rope, but those who are in the business see it as the future, the new gold – the source of a personal fortune. I take it you boys ain't in the fencin' business.'

'No,' Holden replied. 'We're long, experienced cattlemen. Open rangers. Albeit that Judd here has got one of those hundred and sixty-acre homesteads.'

'So, what brings yer two to town, then?' Miss Kittie asked, full of curiosity.

'My hundred and sixty acres,' Judd replied. 'I claimed it under the Homestead Act but it ain't no ordinary homestead. I'm buildin' a town on it called Ramestown, an' we're here to promote that.'

'A town?' Miss Kittie repeated, sounding surprised. 'Ain't never had town promoters pass through here before. This is cattle country.'

'An' like Holden says, we're cattlemen. We first rode the trails goin' north with Charlie Goodnight in '66, an' my town is on one of those trails,' Judd explained. 'It has its own spring an' is at that point north of here when a drover wants to stop, sleep in a decent bed an' have some fun to boot.'

'I must say I ain't heard of it,' Miss Kittie commented.

'Yer'll be hearin' a lot about it, I tell yer,' Judd continued.

'Ramestown is gonna be the cattle town of cattle towns.'

'Guarantee that, can yer mister?' Miss Kittie asked. She had seen plenty of people pass through these parts full of fancy ideas that eventually come to nothing.

'As of yesterday, I believe I can,' said Judd. 'Yer see, yesterday, I signed a contract with the railroad. They are divertin' their line that comes from the southwest to run through Ramestown and then on to the stock town of Kansas where it joins the line running east. It'll cut days off the trail journey from aroun' these parts an' save time an' money gettin' those Texas longhorns to market!'

CHAPTER 1

'Look, here comes another wagon train!' exclaimed Judd, looking out of the second-floor window of the Ramestown Cattlemen's Association building. 'More quitters! Who would have thought our fortunes could have changed so dramatically over seven years! Good job we kept our own herds as an insurance policy, Holden. I have to admit though, I never saw this day comin'!'

Holden joined Judd at the window. 'Oh, it's the Blake family and his followers. He's trouble. Ain't sorry to see him go.'

The two men watched as the small wagon train passed underneath their window and turned right before pulling up outside the coach makers. 'Tryin' to sell some of those wagons no doubt, so they can take the train,' Judd surmised.

'Guess so. Well, they must have checked the new timetable 'cos they picked the right day for the new once-a-week service,' Holden said cynically.

'An' when I think that we used to have a train a day durin' the summer months,' Judd pointed out. 'The railroad put this town on the map an' now it's gonna wipe us off it.'

'Sure looks that way,' Holden agreed. 'Too much track everywhere. No need for long cattle drives anymore to get stock to market. The railroad made us an' it's gonna be the ruin of Ramestown. Let's hope as a farewell gesture it brings in a few people who wanna stay a few nights. I heard Coleman say that he's strugglin' to keep the hotel goin'. He's complainin' about the lack of consistent water supply.'

'There's at least one new homesteader on the inbound train,' Judd remarked. 'Man called Cambray. Mack Cambray and his bride, Effie. He's ridden line fer me a few times. If he ain't too busy, I might wanna use him this winter if he's available to look after my herd.'

'Settlers ain't the solution for this town, though,' Holden interjected. 'In fact, they're part of the problem!' He threw the butt of his cigar angrily out of the window, as if to emphasise his point. 'They stick barbed wire everywhere, makin' it difficult for our cattle to graze the range. Their visits to town ain't that frequent, either: once every few weeks to buy their provisions but they rarely stay an' have a drink or avail themselves of the social facilities.'

'What yer really sayin' is,' Judd said calmly, seeking clarification, 'is that Ramestown was built on one strategic objective and one strategic asset: shortening the length of the cattle trail and the water from the well.'

'The spring water that don't flow regularly anymore,' Holden commented, 'but yes, that's right. The town's prosperity has been too closely tied to the cattle trail an' that's virtually over. Yer lucky if you can afford to hire line riders this winter. I can't. As yer know I'm anti this barbed wire, but I'm gonna have to use it this winter to control my herd: it'll be strung out across my range in a series of unconnected drift fences.'

'Well, my man might be able to advise you on that, but if not,' Judd said, alluding to Holden's customary stubbornness, 'at least he might be able to help us with the spring water issue,' said Judd, looking down at the floor.

'How's that?' Holden asked.

'One of Mack Cambray's many talents is that he's a bit of a water witch. Yer know, a diviner.'

'A diviner, huh?' scoffed Holden Bauldry. 'Well he needs to have more strings to his bow than jest bein' a line rider, I suppose. That's yesterday's job. Yer not much of a man if yer job's been replaced by a bit of barbed wire an' you ain't got nothin' else.'

'Sorry to see that yer leavin', Mr Blake,' said the sheriff, leaning against the wall of his small office, the last building in Main Street, next to the railroad track that ran across the end of the street.

'I thought I would be as well, Sheriff, but I ain't,' Blake replied bitterly. 'Anyways, we ain't as much as leavin', more like we've been driven out!'

'Driven out?' the sheriff queried. 'But by whom an' fer what reason?'

'By Holden Bauldry an' his boys,' Blake spat back. 'They don't recognize my legal rights as a homesteader. I ain't one of those illegal land grabbers, yer know. I got my rights! They think that all this land, as far as the eye can see, is their land to graze their damned cattle on, unrestricted! Don't give a damn about other people's property. If it's in their way, they don't go around it – they jest go through it!'

'Are you sayin' a crime's been committed here, Mr Blake?' the sheriff asked. 'The crime of trespass?'

'Too damned right, that's what I'm sayin', said Blake angrily.

'But you got wire all around your land, ain't yer?' the sheriff asked. 'Barbed wire?'

'Did have,' Blake replied, 'until those critters cut it and allowed their cattle to traipse across my crops an' crush 'em. How am I supposed to feed my family? There's nothin' left!'

'An' how d'yer know it's Bauldry?' the sheriff enquired.

11

'Have yer got any evidence I can go after him with?'

'Only what I saw with my own eyes,' Blake said. 'S'pose that ain't good enough, though.'

'Well, it makes it your word against his,' the sheriff pointed out. 'I'm assumin', of course, that Bauldry would deny the charge.'

'An' you assume correctly, sir!' Blake retorted. ''Cos the likes of Bauldry see 'emselves above the law. And unless you put him in his place, that puts you out of a job as well, 'cos I don't see hordes of cowboys comin' into this town anymore, fer you to keep in check an' justify yer existence!'

Della Peveril awoke from her slumber, slipped on her silk gown and looked out of her window on the top floor of the Ramestown Hotel. She was effectively a permanent resident and, as a long-standing guest, the proprietor had not only given her one of the best rooms in the establishment but also, out of appreciation, only charged her a subsistence rate. It was one of those sunny afternoons in late September that bathed the town in an attractive light, and which by rights should have brought good cheer to Della's spirits. All she could muster, however, was a deep sigh. There was no activity in either Commercial Street or Main Street. Everywhere was dead. There was nothing of interest going on outside to engage Della's imagination and it was hours until show time. Unable to focus on the present and with little to look forward to in the future, her mind began to reflect on the past.

And Della Peveril had a lot to reminisce about, certainly when it came to Ramestown. She first stepped foot in the place when Ramestown was approaching the peak of its fame and fortune. That was five years ago in 1880 when Della was in her early twenties. Born and bred on the eastern seaboard, as a youngster she was a precocious but talented entertainer and her parents sought to underpin this talent with the stability of an education in teaching dance and drama. Her qualification included teaching the educational basics of reading, arithmetic and writing, but after graduation Della had other ideas, and was off west to fulfil her own ambitions in the performing arts. Ramestown became her stage. Whether it was playing the piano in the hotel restaurant or bar, singing Gilbert and Sullivan at the local opera or performing song and dance routines in the Ramestown dance halls, Della was in her element. The hundreds of drovers and cowboys who packed these establishments during the summer months at the end of a trail drive loved to watch Della perform as much as she loved to entertain them. Some evenings she would do six or more shows around the town, hopping from one venue to the next.

But not anymore. Over the last three summers the cattle drives had increasingly tailed off and in the summer of '85 had virtually ceased. Unemployed cowboys could no longer afford to come to town and spend money like it was going out of fashion. Donna was lucky to get one show an evening, let alone six. She knew that it was probably time to move on but the decision to actually leave was a difficult one to make. Ramestown had sentimental value for her; after all it had been her first adult stomping ground. And then there was Dean Comyn, the local, good-looking charmer who worked for Holden Bauldry. Her relationship with Comyn was an on-off one that was on at the moment. She decided she would stay for now and leave next time their relationship was off.

CHAPTER 2

'Ah, this tastes good,' said Mack Cambray, slurping the hot broth from his spoon. 'It's hard work diggin' out that well. Havin' to go down deep, but it'll be worth it.' His wife said nothing. She looked at him and smiled. Water, or the lack of it, was the bane of her life at the moment but she knew that Mack's efforts would be worth it in the long run. Having a large tank of clean water behind their single-storey log house, topped up by a wind pump, would certainly beat catching rainwater off the roof and boiling it by the pot-load to make it safe to drink.

'See anyone while you were in town?' Mack asked.

'Only Judd Rames, husband,' Effie replied. 'Oh, and Della Peveril, who was on the other side of the street. We waved to each other. Judd asked me if you'd made up your mind about his offer to line ride this winter. I told him you'd get back to him in a couple of days. Was that right?'

Mack put down his spoon. 'Yes, Effie, you did well,' he reassured her.

'What will you tell him?'

'My mind says I should go,' Mack replied. 'With the wages, we could afford a wind pump an' that would make such a difference to our lives. Eventually, we would have clean water on tap, enough for cooking and washin' and

14

waterin' the crops as well. Maybe get us some livestock even.'

'You have to work so hard though, husband,' Effie commented. 'I could always sell my music box so you didn't have to go. It would fetch a lot of money back east.'

'No,' said Mack. 'I don't wan' yer to do that. It was a gift from your grandmother, an heirloom, an' I know how much it means to yer. No, if you an' I decide we want the wind pump then I will go an' work for Rames. Mind you, I wouldn't wanna start line ridin' for another few weeks or so. Come what may, I need to take advantage of this dry spell. The water table has dropped lower than normal an' I wanna dig down as deep as I can. Give merself time as well to line the inside with brick and stone, and protect it from any external contamination.'

'You should go then, husband,' Effie advised. 'We owe it to ourselves to cast off as many of the burdens of life as we can. Otherwise this is as good as it gets, an' we sell our potential as people short,' she added philosophically.

'I worry about you, my dear wife,' Mack said. 'I'll be gone from October to spring and if we have a bad winter, it's likely that I'll be cut off and not contactable. It is hard out here bein' on yer own.'

'I will be OK,' Effie reassured him. 'We have enough savings in the bank, so I will be able to eat, and as you know I have a stoic and resolute nature. If I need company, I might cultivate Della Peveril for a friend. I think her and I would get along. I sense she has more depth than her job suggests.'

It was a good few hours later, early evening in fact, when Effie heard a knock on the cabin door. She called out to Mack but received no answer. Assuming that he must be down the well and unable to hear her, she opened the door. She was greeted by two strangers who, judging from their similar wiry physique, she presumed to be cowboys.

However, as they doffed their hats, she could see that one of them was quite a bit younger than the other.

'Good evenin', ma'am,' said the older one with the ice blue eyes. 'Effie Cambray, I presume.'

'Yes, indeed, sir,' Effie replied politely. 'How can I be of assistance?'

'I am Holden Bauldry's operation's manager. This is Holden's nephew, Mose Alder.' The teenage boy barely nodded his head and his shy nature made him look away quickly. The operation's manager cupped his hand against his mouth and spoke softly so Mose couldn't hear. 'The boy's manner is awkward and clumsy. It may make him appear oafish but he is not like that really. Just needs a bit of tough-enin' up, that's all,' he informed Ellie. 'That's why Holden's put him under my charge. But I digress. Our visit is not one of business, ma'am, but social. We come as neighbours, to welcome you and your husband to the neighbourhood.'

'My husband is building a well and is no doubt working at the bottom of the shaft,' Effie explained. 'I will go and get him.' She walked over to the well and, calling down the shaft, advised Mack that they had visitors. The boy followed her over, keen to look down the shaft. His cumbersome gait caused him to kick a plank of wood down the shaft.

'What the. . . ?' Mack shouted out, as the plank narrowly missed his head.

'You stupid boy!' the operation's manager scolded. 'I've told yer to look where you're goin'!' As Mack appeared from the well shaft, the manager's angry demeanour quickly changed to one of calm and courtesy. 'I sincerely apologize, sir, ma'am, for the behaviour of my colleague. I see yer buildin' a well,' he continued. 'Holden told me you're a bit of a water diviner. Is that true?'

'Yep, I guess yer could say that,' Mack replied. 'Learnt a lot from my father. I was raised on the dry plains, as he was, and in order to survive you learn to identify where you might find water.' Effie excused herself to go and pour them all coffee.

'We have a water shortage in Ramestown.' The boy suddenly spoke. 'The spring don't flow like it used to.'

'I expect you need to dig deeper,' Mack said. 'Below the bedrock of the stream. With more settlers, there's a lot of deep wells in the area and when there ain't been rain for a while, it will lower the water table below the bed of the spring.'

'Fascinating,' the operations manager remarked, thinking that here was a man worth keeping in with. 'Yer think you'll get enough water to supply your homestead?' he asked.

'More than enough,' Mack replied. 'I plan to sell what I don't need.'

'Who to?'

'Anyone who wants to buy it: cattlemen, other settlers. . . .'

'Coffee's ready!' Effie called from the cabin door, interrupting the men's conversation. 'Come in an' get it!' The men followed her into the cabin.

'Nice little place you got here, ma'am,' Bauldry's manager commented. 'If yer don't mind me sayin' so.'

'Thank you,' Effie said politely. 'We like it.' She watched the boy as he moved around the table and over to the mantelpiece. His eyes set on her music box. If she was worried that he might pick it up and clumsily drop it in the floor, she needn't have. As he ran his fingers gently over its fine surface she saw a change in his demeanour. The awkwardness of adolescence was replaced suddenly by self-confidence, the maturity and sophistication of an admirer of fine things.

'It's beautiful,' he whispered in awe. 'The craftsmanship,

17

the creativity.' Effie smiled at him.

'You seem to have an understanding of the skills and effort required to make this,' Effie said, trying not to sound too surprised.

'Only a little, ma'am. I – I try to carve myself,' the boy replied. He produced a small wooden block from his pocket, upon the surface of which he had etched an eagle's head skilfully.

'That is very good,' Effie said slightly taken aback that this seemingly oafish boy had produced something so intricate. The boy blushed as his shyness returned. Effie distracted his attention away from himself and back to the music box.

'Listen, Mose,' she said and wound the handle on the side of the small cabinet. The music box started to gently play.

'I've heard this tune before,' he said. 'I like it.'

'It's *Für Elise*,' Effie told him. 'Beethoven.'

'It is wonderful. Truly wonderful,' the boy muttered as he moved back to the table where the men were sitting and talking.

'So yer plannin' to ride the line for Judd, then?'

'Well, that's the plan,' Mack said, 'but I need to let Effie give it her full consideration first before I tell Judd. I'll be away for some months.'

'I'm afraid we need to be movin' on,' the operation's manager said, 'but let me know if you decide to ride the line. I'd be happy to look in on your good lady occasionally if that would make you both feel more comfortable.'

'That's very kind of you, sir,' said Effie, catching the tail end of the men's conversation.

'It's what good neighbours do. Thanks for the coffee and see you both soon. C'mon boy, time to go!'

As they ate their supper that night, Mack asked Effie what she thought of their early evening guests.

'Complete opposites,' she remarked with a slight chuckle. 'As awkward and introverted as the boy was, the man was outgoing and charming. I know the boy's name is Mose but I didn't catch the man's name. Did he tell you what it is?'

'Yes,' Mack replied. 'It's Dean Comyn.'

CHAPTER 3

Mack Cambray looked up at the winter sky. Bathed in an even, deep, grey wash and full of snow, it gave the range an air of foreboding. He dismounted from his horse and opened the door of his one-room log cabin on the eastern side of the valley. He had spent the latter part of the afternoon plugging the gaps between the planks with foliage, twigs and mud, as much as he could lay his hands on. It was New Year's Eve and his knowledge of the range and his senses told him that the start to 1886 was not going to be a pleasant one. *The cattle know*, he thought to himself. *They know.*

All day long he had watched them slowly drifting south, driven by their instincts that something from the north was coming to get them. He couldn't stop their movement south but as a line rider he could round up the strays and try and stop the southern edge of the herd from breaking up. Riding the line, Mack was used to working outside when it was bitterly cold, but if a blizzard were to start he knew he would be better off hunkered down in his cabin than trying to be a hero out on the range. Besides, his was likely the only intact and serviceable line rider's dwelling for some way and it would be extremely difficult trying to find shelter if caught outside in a rough storm.

It never used to be that way. Line riders used to be an essential resource for a successful open range cattle operation but, since the advent of barbed wire, many cattlemen had decided it would be cheaper to build drift fences across the range – unconnected lines of barbed wire to keep the herd together and save a fortune in wages. Unusually, Holden Bauldry was in this new camp, whereas Judd Rames, on Mack's advice, was in the traditional one. Mack hoped for everyone's sake that his advice wasn't going to be tested.

As the last of the daylight started to fade away, he laid out his bedding on the cabin floor and lit the stove. Mack held the stove door open and watched the flames as they flickered more or less evenly in the grate. *That was good*, he thought to himself. It meant that he had plugged most of the gaps in the walls of the cabin, which would help prevent the winter wind swirling around inside.

He had checked the roof of the cabin just the other week. The other two line riders, Judd Rames' eldest and youngest sons, laughed at his thoroughness. He had not only inspected the underside, but had also climbed on top and tested the soundness of the structure. Not a particularly easy job, given the steep pitch and the tin sheet covering, but both features would help a heavy snowfall to slide off rather than put excessive burden on the cabin's frame. The roof extended beyond the edge of the living area to make a porch over the southerly-facing front door and a stall for a couple of horses with a storage area for their hay. The cabin had been specially designed for the needs of a line rider and Mack knew from experience that, if maintained properly, it would provide protection from extreme weather conditions.

Finally, he made a last check on his food supplies. He had learnt this lesson the hard way when once, during a few days of heavy snow, he had started preparing a meal only to find that rodents had got into his shelter and been feasting on

21

some of his provisions. The pitch of the roof provided a useful storage area in the form of a small loft where he kept his larder, which consisted of several days' supply of fresh meat that he had cut into thin, heavily-salted strips and wrapped in a vinegar soaked cloth, plus hardtack and dried fruit. And if that ran out before he could get the chance to replace it, he had some canned food including vegetables, meat and condensed milk.

He brewed himself a cup of coffee and perched on top of his bedding. He wondered how Effie was. He had sent her a letter with a small item of jewellery he had picked up in a watch repairer's in the nearest town about a day's ride away. He had posted it at the local Wells Fargo office and they had assured him that it would reach her by Christmas. That was mid-December. Apart from talking to himself occasionally, that was the last time he had spoken to anyone. He poured a tot of whiskey into his coffee and thought about settling down for the night.

Half a mile or so further west, by the creek, Judd Rames' eldest son, Pete, was going through similar preparations, albeit not quite the same as Mack. Never one to go hungry, his main focus was on the quality of his food supplies rather than that of his shelter, although he did carry out a visual inspection of its key structural components. A similar distance away from Pete but in a southwesterly direction, on the far side of the valley, Pete's young brother, Judd junior, was following a slightly different regime from his two colleagues. Having spent the majority of his food money on bottles of whiskey, he reasoned that he could live off his emergency canned food supplies for that short period while the threatened storm passed over.

In normal conditions, the three line riders between them could close off the southern section of the valley and keep the herd together north of an imaginary line linking their three cabins. But with the heavens above them about to open, the one thing that all three line riders could agree on was that attending to their own personal preparations had become priority over stopping the herd from straying. Once the storm started, they all knew that the herd would head south in its search for shelter.

Mack had drifted off to sleep fairly easily but was awoken a few hours later by the sound of the howling wind. It was dark outside and he got up off his bed and poked at the glowing embers in the grate of the stove. Stirred from their slumber, they spat and glowed as they came to life. He threw a couple of small dry logs on top and, crouching down on his haunches, waited until they caught fire. The increase in light from the stove enabled Mack to take a quick look around the cabin. Everything seemed fine; there were no drips of water coming from the loft area or the roof. He looked at his shirt, which he had hung up on a washing line strung across the far end of the cabin. There was no movement – it hung perfectly still. Mack took satisfaction in his earlier efforts to weatherproof the cabin.

He peered out of the window. The ground was now a blanket of white snow, and against the dark backcloth of the night sky all he could see was a hypnotic, ever changing swirl of dancing snowflakes. Looking along the length of the cabin beneath the window, he could tell from the lie of the snow that it was starting to drift up against the back wall. He decided to venture outside and check his horse. Opening the front door, he was still able to step out onto the narrow veranda that ran the length of the small stable next to it and, thanks to the southerly facing aspect of this area with its extended gable roof, enjoy reasonable protection from the ravages of the blizzard. He peered through the small side window into his horse's stall. The animal looked OK.

'Looks like this might be it fer a few days,' Mack muttered to himself. 'Guess I'm jest gonna have to sit it out.'

What with being a good sleeper anyway, the few glasses of whiskey that Pete drank before he went to bed that night ensured that he didn't wake up until mid-morning the next day. Not normally much of a drinker, the one thing that would keep Pete awake at night was the noise of a storm. And the harder he tried to go to sleep, the longer he would lie awake wondering what damage the storm might be doing to his property. The brief periods of silence seemed to amplify the intermittent howling of the wind. But over the years, he had found that a pretty good cure was a few jars of whiskey before bedtime and then to wait for the numbing effect of the alcohol on his senses.

Ironically, he was awakened by the after-effect of some minor damage to his property: the steady drip of ice cold water on his face. Slowly, he rubbed his eyes and opened them. Although mentally he felt slightly jaded from last night's whiskey, and physically down on his energy levels, he certainly could not be described as out.

'Damn!' he said out loud. He looked above him and saw there were a number of drips coming through between the roof boards. He got to his feet and started to move quickly. He dragged his bed across the cabin and sited it under the loft shelving area, where his food was stored. That sorted the problem of having somewhere dry to sleep but it would probably mean having to move his larder down from the loft. Pete rigged up the small wooden ladder that he kept inside the cabin and took a look. As he expected, water was dripping through the roof boards in quite a number of places, including on his provisions. He moved them down hastily and placed them under his bed.

He then needed to fix the cause of these problems. He reasoned, correctly, that the tin sheeting which covered the roof boards must have blown away, and the warm air in the cabin was finding its way through the gaps in the roof boards and starting to melt the snow slowly. Pete rummaged around in the drawer of the small cupboard where he kept his pots and pans and found a small tin of nails and a hammer. All he needed to do was go outside and retrieve the tin sheets. He looked out of the small cabin window to see if he could find them. The view made him feel slightly queasy: there was no horizon, no identifiable objects to focus on. Everything was white. It was as if a white ghost had stood outside and painted the pane of glass white.

His preferred avenue of repair was clearly not open to him; Pete knew that he needed to come up with another solution. The obvious one was to turn off the stove so that the snow stopped melting, but that would mean sleeping in freezing temperatures, which would greatly reduce his chances of survival. As he placed his pots and pans under the heavier drips, his mind worked on the problem. 'I know,' he said to himself. 'There will be earth under the floor-boards. As soon as the storm abates, I'll clear the snow from the roof, nail some oilcloth over the gaps then plug them from inside with mud. The heat from the stove should dry that out before it snows again!' He went out to the stable, where he kept the oilcloth, and grabbed a shovel to lever up a floorboard.

Judd junior lay on his bed. He was starting to go stir crazy. He had been stuck in this damned line rider's cabin for a number of days now and the blizzard had still not shown any real signs of abating. And then there was the gnawing effect of hunger. He had been living off half rations for a while but was out of food. The lack of decent sustenance and the excess of whiskey had made him feel a little lightheaded. He knew that half a mile away to the west, the uplands began: foothills, some of them forested, the entrance to the mountainous area beyond. There one might find elk, mountain lion, bear even. Judd salivated at the thought of a bear steak.

He looked out of his window towards the west. Could he make out the shape of the foothills through the driving snow? No, but wait! There was something out there that seemed to be moving, coming nearer even. Judd wanted to get closer to the window, but every time he did so his warm breath misted the ice-cold pane of glass. He wiped the pane clear with his cuff.

'I must be seeing things,' he muttered to himself. 'It can't be, surely.' He peered closer in an attempt to confirm if his eyes and brain were trying to deceive him or not. 'No, it damn well is!' he shouted, 'It's a bear!' He went and grabbed his rifle. 'Must be lost,' he muttered, 'and looking for food. Well, Mr Bear, so am I.'

Judd rushed outside into the blinding snow. It was a total whiteout. He looked to where he thought he had seen the bear, a slightly greyer, off-white shape amidst the swirling, white flakes. Nothing. He waded through the drifting snow to the window and took up the same position from where he had observed the creature when inside the cabin. He blasted off a couple of rounds. Through the howling wind he thought he heard a cry – a death cry!

'Gotcha!' he exclaimed and raced as fast as he could towards his kill.

CHAPTER 4

As she watched the snow from her window, Effie wondered how Mack must have been making out on the exposed prairie. The snow was falling thick and fast on their homestead so she knew that conditions must be a lot harsher out on the ranges. However, her Mack was a man who knew how to look after himself: courageous but not foolhardy, principled yet pragmatic. As she looked out of her window at the dark night, she thought she could make out the figure of a stranger amidst the swirling snow making their way up the path. She wondered if it was just an illusion – in the same way that it is possible to see shapes in the clouds, so it is in wind driven snow. The loud knock on the door confirmed that what she saw was real.

'Oh, it's you,' she said in a disheartened tone. Even if he noticed, Dean Comyn was too cocksure of himself to be put off by such a slight, knowing that his natural charm would soon win her round and reverse any negative sentiment.

'Evenin', Miss Effie,' he said, with a smile on his face and a sparkle in his eye. She held the door open wide, a signal for him to step across the threshold. Whatever it was he wanted to say, she knew that he wasn't going to go away until he had said it and it would be far more comfortable having the conversation in front of a warm fire rather than on an

27

icy, cold doorstep.

'Jest passin', he continued taking off his hat. 'Thought I'd look in on you. It's gonna be a bad night. This storm don't look like its gonna pass anytime soon. Is the coffee pot on?'

'Yes,' Effie said. 'You ... you'd like a cup?' she asked slightly nervously, hoping that, given the extreme weather, he wouldn't misinterpret any gesture of hospitality as an invitation to stay the night. As she poured the coffee, she wondered what was making her think that way. After all, it was perfectly socially acceptable under the circumstances, an unwritten rule in fact, that even a woman living on her own might give a male, whether an acquaintance or stranger, shelter from the storm. Such an invitation would not have been an act of disloyalty to her new friend, Della, or her husband. One never knew, in the unforgiving environment of the western frontier, when one might be only too glad to call upon another's hospitality. She decided that perhaps she should be more accommodating and smiled warmly as she passed him his coffee.

'Thank you, Miss Effie,' Dean said, gratefully. 'I'm chilled to the bone. Do yer have a little tot of something I could put in it?'

'Yes,' she replied. 'Whiskey OK?'

'Most definitely,' Dean said. While Effie went to the dresser to fetch the whiskey bottle, he took off his gloves and laid them on the table. He then removed his cloak, but as he turned to hang it behind the door, along with his hat, he managed to knock one of the gloves onto the floor without realizing.

'Here, help yourself,' Effie said generously, as she turned around and passed him the bottle.

'Why, thank you, Miss Effie. Very kind of you,' Dean said, feeling that she was trying to make amends for her initial frostiness by making him feel more welcome. He found this woman difficult to fathom. She seemed to blow hot and cold towards him. It was as if on occasion she could see right through him and he stood naked, regardless of how he tried to dress himself up. Maybe she was his nemesis. The very thought sent a visible shudder down his spine. 'Cold gone right through to me bones,' he said, in case she had noticed. *As if she could read my mind*, he thought to himself. *C'mon, get a grip, Comyn.*

It was difficult for him. He liked both Effie and her husband Mack, and his original offer to look in on her while Mack was away riding the line had been a genuine one. Although he barely knew Mack, he had warmed to him and his seemingly innovative spirit – a true man of the frontier. And as a woman, the more he saw of Effie, the more attractive he found her and indeed, if she were to lead him on, he knew that he wouldn't be able to stop himself taking advantage of the opportunity. But as much as that temptation would have been welcome it seemed increasingly unlikely and, the more he saw of her, he sensed that she was purposely creating an ever-widening gulf between them. Still, that was by the by. His real motive for visiting Miss Effie, as he enjoyed calling her, was of a business nature rather than a social one, and there was work to be done. His boss, Holden Bauldry, wanted information and would pay Dean handsomely for it, in addition to the execution of any action that he deemed necessary that resulted from it.

Holden Bauldry's philosophy was quite simple. The cattlemen were on the range before the homesteaders, and the fact that so many of the American population enjoyed their beef justified the right of the cattlemen to stay there and carry on in the ways they had fashioned. The arrival of settlers, encouraged by the federal government, generally undermined this right by creating competition for key resources such as land and water. By default, a lawmaking and enforcement process that often occurred after the event – rather than pre-empting it – had helped create a war of attrition between the two parties. The latest battleground was the settlers' use of barbed wire, which they used to fence in their land, but in so doing often restricted the cattlemen's access to parts of the range where the herds could feed and drink.

As far as Holden was concerned, settlers with barbed wire fencing were potential targets. First of all, they needed to be leaned on to see if they would cave in under pressure, such as the Blake family, or stand their ground. Then, for those that stood their ground, Holden would seek to negotiate some sort of settlement such as agreeing a right of way through a homestead claim for the cattlemen. Dealing with settlers was Dean's job and Holden made it clear to him that he didn't condone violence in its execution; a negotiated deal could always be found somehow and consequently, in principle at least, was preferable to no deal.

Dean had reported back that the Cambrays were firmly in the 'stand their ground' camp, but with the husband's knowledge of water sources and their management he thought that this might be a fruitful area for negotiation.

As he poured a tot of whiskey into his coffee and roasted his feet at her hearth, Effie suddenly realized what her problem was with her guest. It was Comyn's obvious pleasure in calling her Miss Effie. She wasn't Miss Effie to him or anyone else for that matter. As far as she was concerned, she wasn't even Mrs Effie Cambray to him anymore; she was plain Mrs Cambray. It was that continuous, undiluted flow of smarmy charm that angered her. Where was the sincerity, the integrity? This man had visited her a number of times now and he seemed just an empty shell, with no depth and no real values. All he wanted to do was to ask questions, as if

slowly peeling the layers off her personality to expose her
true motivations underneath. But what for? Could she trust
him? The incessant and repeated questions about her
husband's potential foray into the water supply business,
and about her resolve to make a go of it in the west. What
business was it of his?

'I'll fix your fence once the storm passes,' Dean said,
interrupting her thoughts. 'Was gonna do it last week, like I
promised, but I ran out of time,' he continued. 'Gotta lot of
work on at the moment, yer see. . . .' If he wasn't grilling her
with questions, she had to listen to his monologues about
himself and this one, which was supposed to be an apology,
didn't even contain the word 'sorry'. The fence, yes, she
thought to herself. The mystery of the cut fence, the tram-
pled crops, and the silence afterwards – nobody heard
anything and nobody saw anything. Except Dean offered to
fix it. Yet she hadn't even told him about it. Later she found
out that Della had mentioned it to him. Although no one
witnessed this intentional act of violation of her property,
some were prepared to offer advice.

'Beware, Mrs Cambray: there have been a number of
fence cutting violations lately,' they told her. 'That's what
made up the Blakes' minds to leave when it happened to
them.' She'd heard the stories around town about the
Blake's sudden departure and how they had pointed the
finger at Holden Bauldry. So was Dean Comyn actually the
fence cutter and, on behalf of Bauldry, testing her resilience
to stay? When she stood her ground, was his offer to fix it an
attempt not to blow his cover? Or was she just being para-
noid?

Effie got up from her chair as Comyn refilled his empty
coffee cup with another large slug of whiskey. She thought
quickly. 'When you've drained the contents of that cup and
warmed yourself sufficiently to face the elements again, I'd

like you to leave, please,' she said firmly but politely. 'It's been a long day and I want to turn in.'

'But Miss Effie,' he interjected, looking concerned. It was difficult to tell whether his look of concern was caused by the realization that he may have overstayed his welcome or because he might not be able to achieve his personal agenda for the evening. 'This whiskey gone to me head a bit. I'd be grateful if you could make me another pot of coffee; help me sober up a little first.' Effie reached in the pocket of dress.

It was difficult to tell whether he was bluffing or not. Effie didn't think he seemed drunk, although he may have started slurring the occasional word. But if he didn't go now, Effie reasoned, he would almost certainly sit there and work his way through the rest of that bottle and undoubtedly end up drunk. And what kind of drunk would he turn out to be, an amorous one or a fighting one? She pulled her handkerchief from her dress pocket and mopped her brow delicately. Comyn just sat there, not really knowing what to make of the situation. He watched her put the handkerchief back in her pocket and leave her hand in there. He thought nothing of it.

It was when she took it out again that he started thinking and double fast. Wrapped in Effie's delicate palm was a pocket Derringer – the lady's gun. 'I would like you to leave now,' she said, as cold as ice. Dean Comyn jumped to his feet. She had outwitted him!

'You bitch!' he screamed at the top of his voice.

CHAPTER 5

It took several long days for the storm to stop, but as soon as it did Mack was outside at first light checking the external structure of his cabin. Although the snow had drifted more than six feet high against the back wall, the structure of the cabin was sound, as was that of the attached small stable. Inside generally, and particularly in the loft area, he found no signs of any leaks. He went outside again and took a look at the sky. It was turning blue as the sun rose and, although Mack realized that the blizzard could return, it wouldn't be for at least several hours. That would give him time to check on the Rames brothers and, if needs be, make it back to his own cabin.

Having enjoyed a hearty breakfast, he packed half his remaining provisions in his saddlebag. Grabbing his rifle and a spade he saddled his horse and, using the sun as his compass, headed out west towards Pete Rames' cabin. The deep snow slowed their progress and Mack was able to ride his horse at little more than walking pace, but he had factored this into calculations along with several other contingencies.

The one contingency he hadn't factored in was the sight that greeted him as Pete Rames' cabin came into view. At first Mack wondered if it was some sort of illusion created by the reflective surface of the snow. That turned out to be wishful thinking, however, because as he got closer he could see that the middle section of the cabin appeared to have fallen down, with smoke rising from the ruins. He pulled his rifle out of its holster, in case there had been some sort of foul play and its perpetrators were still in the area. Cold, hunger and dehydration can make the most honourable of men resort to behaviours that they would have others strung up for.

'Mack!' He heard Pete Rames call out. In the distance, he could make out waving arms.

'What happened?' Mack asked as he dismounted.

'Damn cabin roof started collapsin' a few days ago,' Pete replied. Wrapped in a dry blanket, he was trying to keep warm by the fire. 'Final bit fell last night. Weight of snow on it . . . Fortunately, the snow was easin' up then. This damned blanket and meself are about the only things that have survived. Few cans of food as well, but that's about it. The bed's on the fire. I managed to get the wet mattress to catch light eventually. Created a lot of smoke, yer see, an' I was hopin' that someone might see it an' come lookin' fer me. Had almost given up hope, an' then out of the blue, you arrive.'

'What about yer horse?' Mack said.

'Bolted when the roof started collapsin'. God only knows where he's gone,' Pete replied. 'I didn't know what to do for the best, stay put or try an' find you or Judd junior. What would you have done, Mack?'

'Stayed put,' said Mack, not wishing to query how well Pete may have attempted to storm-proof his cabin. 'But I would probably have dug merself a snow cave straight away and slept in there in the warm, rather than havin' a few sleepless nights wonderin' when the whole roof might fall on my head.'

'Guess yer right, guess yer right,' Pete replied. 'So what now?'

'I'm not sure that we can salvage enough materials to rebuild an adequate shelter,' Mack remarked, 'an' even if we were able to there might be a follow up blizzard. Pretty common in these parts. Could take too much time to repair this place and make it storm-proof, an' we don't wanna get caught out.'

'So, what yer suggest?' Pete asked.

'We continue headin' west,' Mack replied. 'Check out yer little brother's place. See if he's all right. If yer still got any food that's usable, gather it together an' we'll take it with us.' The two men climbed on his horse and started their journey to Judd junior's cabin.

'What's that over there, lyin' in the snow?' Pete asked as he looked over Mack's shoulder and pointed in a northwesterly direction. Mack stopped the horse and looked to where Pete was pointing.

'Dunno, let's take a look,' he replied, pulling lightly on the rein to encourage his horse to change direction. They rode for another hundred yards or so in silence until the object lying in the snow became distinguishable.

'It's a dead horse,' Mack said.

'It's my horse!' Pete exclaimed. They dismounted and took a closer look. Strips of flesh had been torn savagely from the animal, revealing the bone in places.

'That's a bear done that,' Mack pointed out. 'We're near bear country out here. In this weather, they'll come down out of the mountains hungry, lookin' anywhere for food. Yer horse was probably already dead by the time the bear had a go at it. C'mon, let's get goin',' Mack urged. 'There ain't nothin' we can do for it.'

It was late afternoon when they approached Judd junior's cabin from the east side and the light was starting to fade. There was no smoke coming from the chimney, which both men thought odd. They went inside and found the fire in the grate was out. The ashes were barely warm to touch. The place looked a bit of a mess: empty whiskey bottles lying on the floor, no food left and no Judd. The two men looked at each other concerned as they read the ominous signs.

'I'll check the stable,' said Pete, in a very matter of fact way. Mack looked around the cabin to see what else might be missing. 'Horse is still in the stable an' seems to be OK,' Pete said as he came back into the cabin.

'Rifle's missin',' said Mack. 'Maybe he went huntin' fer food.'

'That bear that got my horse?' Pete pondered.

'Could be,' Mack replied while walking out onto the veranda. He lit a match. 'There's footprints down here. Need a lantern to see them properly. Should be some up in the loft area.' Pete went and retrieved a couple and, once he had got one of them to light, joined Mack on the veranda. They studied the footprints.

'They're deep,' Mack observed, 'but there's powdered snow lying in the bottom of 'em.' He bent down and put his hand in. 'This powdered snow's about six inches deep. I reckon these footprints were made while the storm was still ragin' but not that long before it started easin' up.'

'What, like earlier on last night?' Pete suggested.

'Yep, could well be.'

'Well, they obviously belong to my brother, an' if we're right about the time they were made that means he could still be out there alive.'

'Yep,' said Mack. 'Let's see if we can follow 'em, but first we should light the other lantern and place it in the cabin window so that we can easily find our way back.'

As they followed the footprints, Judd's journey into the snow became more and more curious. Starting at the end of the veranda it appeared that he had walked along the side of the cabin up to the window before turning ninety degrees and heading out west into the wilderness of the prairie.

'What d'yer make of that?' Pete asked.

'Looks to me as if he had been lookin' out of the window, thought he saw somethin' and wanted to confirm that he was settin' out in the right direction towards whatever it was,' Mack suggested.

'A bear?'

'Possibly,' Mack replied. As they pursued the footprints out on to the prairie, they found that drifting snow had covered some of them. However, with the aid of the lantern, they were able to look around that point and pick up the trail again.

'There's his rifle!' Pete exclaimed suddenly. He waded towards where it had been stuck in the snow, butt first, its barrel pointing up towards the sky. 'Strange to leave the rifle here, an' in that position,' he commented.

'Maybe he was usin' it at as a marker. Look, the footprints go beyond it an' then start turnin' back on themselves, but heading in a new direction.'

'What about the bear?'

'Maybe there wasn't a bear; maybe he'd had a hallucination,' Mack said. 'Can easily happen in a snowstorm cos it's so easy to lose direction, especially if you're hungry an' been drinkin' as well.'

Instinctively, Pete looked back to the lantern light in the cabin window. 'An' knowin' my brother, he probably didn't think to put a light in the window as a navigation aid. Jest used that damned stupid rifle. It's true ain't it that, when lost, people often walk around in a big circle?'

' 'Fraid so,' said Mac. ' 'Fraid so,' he repeated as Judd's trail turned again, suggesting that that was what had happened to him. Indeed, after another twenty minutes or so of tracking, the slowly turning trail started to lead them back to the north-facing back wall of the cabin. It was five minutes later that they found Judd junior's frozen dead body, lying face down in the snowdrift that had piled up against the back wall.

CHAPTER 6

Della Peverell sat on the bed studying her array of contracts for the various entertainment spots. She still had one or two residences going but even those had the same clause: if crowd numbers fell below a certain level then her regular fixed wages stopped and her income was based on a small percentage of the takings. One of her residencies had already invoked that clause and she expected the place she was playing tonight, Jim's, would do the same. The alternative offered by these establishments' owners was to forgo the percentage and rely on having an empty beer jug passed around and taking what the patrons decided to put in it. A good deal perhaps, in the summer season, when the cowboys were flush with money after working the trails but not out of season and certainly not in this current economic downturn that had hit Ramestown. A girl could live off cash but not off the half-finished cigarettes, silver bullets and lucky rabbit's feet that the punters would throw in the jug rather than give up any of their beer money. Still, it was show time in an hour and she needed to get ready and walk out on that stage feeling and looking like she was worth a million dollars.

As she put on her make-up, Della started rehearsing the songs that she was going to perform that night. Trooper that she was, she soon forgot about her financial plight, and willed that million-dollar feeling back. Her transition was cut short by an unexpected loud banging on the door. The suddenness of the interruption jarred, just as it did when a drunk in the audience started heckling. Della would normally deal with that situation by making a few humorous comments deprecating their manhood, but she suspected that might be inappropriate on this occasion and that she should attend to her caller.

'Hi, hon, it's me.' Dean Comyn barged his way into her room and shut the door behind him. 'Gotta bit of a problem I need you to help me with,' he explained before she could say anything. 'Had to collect a small but long outstanding gambling debt this evening. Unfortunately, the debtors were not at home so I broke in and took a few bits and pieces of equivalent value.'

'Will they come after you?' Della asked, sounding concerned. 'Will they know it's you?'

'They'll work that out but they're too soft to come after me. No, they'll go to the sheriff and say I burgled them. So if the sheriff drops by and asks you anything about my whereabouts, tell 'im that I've been here with you all night. Oh, and look after that for me.' From behind his back he produced a small brown paper bag, which contained what looked like a small box wrapped in black tissue paper and pushed it towards her.

'What's this?' Effie asked, taking hold of the bag.

'Don't know exactly,' Dean replied. 'Some fancy box of trinkets, I think, all part of their debt. Anyway, lock it in the bottom of your trunk an' don't let anybody see it. Don't worry, I'll square it away with the sheriff in the fullness of time,' he explained, opening the door. 'Gotta go,' he said, blowing her kiss as he shut the door.

'Hm,' Della sighed as she put the bag in her trunk. Life with Dean was never boring but she needed to forget about his antics right now. Her number one priority was to prepare herself to deliver another top-drawer performance.

It had just turned half past midnight when Della came off stage to a standing ovation.

'That was great, Della,' the proprietor said as he greeted her in the wings. 'Here's your percentage and as a bonus we decided to pass the jug round so there's a few dollars more.'

'Why, thanks, Jim,' she said, smiling. 'I'll treat merself to a nightcap before I leave.'

'What would you like?' he asked.

'A brandy would be nice,' she replied.

'Comin' up and on the house!' the proprietor said. Della never gave a bad performance. She was too professional for that but tonight she knew that she had really nailed it. She'd sung well, she looked good and she felt good – like a million dollars. She sat at a small round table at the end of the bar where she was unlikely to be disturbed, but could eavesdrop the nearby conversations and not only revel in any praise being bandied around about her performance, but also pick up on any negative comments. It was a useful way of understanding her audience and what they liked and what they didn't.

'Hear Dean Comyn's been arrested,' one voice said. Della's ears pricked up at the mention of the man's name. Instinctively, she drained her glass.

'It's serious,' another voice said.

'Why? What's he supposed to have done?' someone else asked.

'He's been charged with the murder of Effie Cambray,' the first voice replied. Della felt a sudden rush of adrenaline and a sinking feeling in the pit of her stomach.

'You all right, Miss Della?' the proprietor enquired.

'Yes, I'm fine, thanks Jim,' Della replied, regaining her

composure. 'Can yer put one for the road in there?' she said, offering him her empty glass.

CHAPTER 7

The next day, Pete Rames and Mack buried the body of Pete's younger brother, Judd junior. Judd's chosen lifestyle had put him on a difficult path that had extended as far as his death. Where the snow cover was at its shallowest and it was possible to find the ground underneath, the topsoil was frozen, which made digging the grave backbreaking work. Eventually, after several hours, Pete and Mack managed to hollow out a small trench and bury the body deep enough so that it would not be discovered and dug up again by a wild animal.

Pete gave a short but touching eulogy about how it wasn't Judd junior's youthful zest for life that determined that his would be a short one but, like many young people before him and no doubt after him, it was Judd's belief that he was invincible. In spite of the fact that his body was not immortal, his soul however, was eternal and would enable poor Judd junior to rest in peace.

After the service ended they went inside the cabin and started to make plans. Mack found a map of the surrounding area in amongst Judd's meagre possessions and proceeded to spend some time studying it.

'What's got yer interest?' Pete asked.

'Lookin' at this, I think I can see where our cattle might be,' Mack answered. Pete put his coffee down and came and looked over Mack's shoulder.

'I reckon we're about here, virtually on the edge of the prairie,' Mack said, pointing at the map. 'And here, not far to our west, is the hill country with the mountains behind them, as you can see marked. Then, if you go southwest from where we are, you come to this outcrop of rocks and caves that marks the southern end of the mountains. I reckon it's five miles away at the most. According to this map there are caves and streams there, the ideal place for cattle to take shelter. I'd bet money that's where we might find whatever might be left of our herd, given that many of the weaker animals would have died on the way.'

'You're thinking we should go down there an' take a look?' Pete asked.

'Yep,' Mack replied. 'We could go tomorrow if the weather still looks favourable.'

'An' if we get there and the blizzard starts again?'

'There must be plenty of places to shelter if there are caves there. We'll have to live off the land, no doubt, but there should be a choice of meat to hunt, be it bear, elk or mountain lion. And we can protect the herd from those creatures as well. They'll be isolating the weaker ones and feedin' off the stragglers in the herd.'

'OK,' said Pete thoughtfully. 'Yep, it makes sense. If the opportunity presents itself, let's take it.' He stopped and thought for a while. 'I wonder how Holden Bauldry's makin' out,' he said. 'Holden ain't used line riders like us this year. He's gone for drift fences made of barbed wire to control his herds. What'd yer think?'

'My bet is he ain't makin' out at all,' Mack said. 'I reckon he's probably lost most of his herd. But time will tell, once the snows start meltin'.'

It was another few weeks before that happened and the cattlemen could traverse the range again. In the interim, Mack

44

and Pete had found the core of the herd where they had suspected, but not only did another blizzard set in during that time, it was quickly followed by a third storm. As the snow finally started melting, however, Pete made the journey northeast alone to break the bad news to his father about Judd junior, while Mack stayed with the herd to await advice from the Rames family as to where they wanted them moved.

Pete's journey back was slow, uneventful and boring. Apart from the occasional bird, the prairie was empty and silent, with most of the land still asleep under its white blanket. An air of serenity pervaded the stillness, as if the world was at peace with itself. It lulled Pete into a false sense of security, leaving him completely unprepared for what awaited him as he reached the southern edge of what was known locally as Bauldry's Prairie.

Pete Rames was physically sick as he looked at the scene of devastation spread out before him. Cattle that had frozen to death were huddled up against each other all along the barbed wire drift fence. Some looked as if they had been suffocated and trodden on by those who had been behind them. Away from the drift fences he found others, drowned but with missing limbs, amputated by the ice where they had attempted to cross frozen streams. It would have been a lucky few that had been able to skirt around the end of the drift fences and not die of exposure from the forces of Mother Nature.

CHAPTER 8

As Ramestown stood on the edge of potentially terminal decline, Wells Fargo put its own particular nail in the coffin and reduced the daily stage coach service to twice a week, with the service east leaving at the ungodly time of sunrise, and the one west leaving half an hour later. The second service of the week in question left on the morning following Della Peveril's successful performance at Jim's saloon, and she was determined she was going to be on it in spite of little sleep that night. The Wells Fargo office was opposite her hotel so she had arranged for her bags and trunk to be ferried across the road by one of the Wells Fargo clerks.

Her slight quandary was whether to return home and take the stage east or settle for the great unknown and take the one going west. When she arrived at the office, the eastbound stage was in and loading but, as the clerk explained, was already fully booked. He said he could guarantee her a ticket to the end of the line going west, however, an offer that she accepted gladly. After all, in spite of the sudden upset for Della, the west still represented, freedom, fun and opportunity whereas the east was about servility, drudgery and knowing your place in the class system.

She had a small amount of savings, so new directions and new beginnings were very much the order of the day for her

46

now. She was sad to leave Ramestown in many ways but desperate to get away from that no-good lowlife Dean Comyn, who had tried to con her into lying for him and incriminating herself into the bargain just so that he could get off a murder rap! She seethed with anger every time she thought about it and promised herself that once she was beyond the town limits, she would let it go and stop thinking about it.

A few hundred yards away, around the corner at the bottom of Main Street, Dean Comyn had also had a sleepless night and was similarly seething with anger. Not only had Sheriff McMaster brought in a meagre breakfast but seemed to enjoy rubbing salt in the wound by sitting and explaining what would probably happen next.

'Jest managin' your expectations, Comyn, that's all I'm doin',' he said. 'Wouldn't be right if you weren't made aware, now, would it? But for starters, I wanna point out that you're in enough trouble as it is, so I wouldn't let your anger go getting the better of you.'

'I jest wanna know if Bauldry's gonna stand me bail an' I can get out of here!' Dean retaliated.

'From what I know of Holden Bauldry, I don't think he likes gettin' mixed up in stuff like this. No profit in it fer him, yer see,' the sheriff explained. 'Besides, I don't think the US Commissioner would wanna allow you bail. The penalty aroun' these parts for what you're accused of is death, an' a man with the weight of that thought on his mind could well be tempted to skip bail. But don't you fear. The law will see to it that yer get a fair trial, even if you plead not guilty. Be a trial by jury, no doubt. You'll be judged by yer peers. They're unlikely to be from aroun' these parts, though. Too many people know yer aroun' here, an' if they happen not to like yer as well, they might assume you're guilty automatically.'

Dean Comyn opened his mouth to say something but bit his tongue. He just sneered instead. He wasn't going to let this sheriff wind him up. He looked down at the floor. 'Got any smokes?' he asked in a civil voice.

'Sure,' said Sheriff McMaster, satisfied that he'd put his prisoner in his place. 'Here, have the rest of the packet. You're gonna be in here for a good few days before yer trial starts an' you might be glad of a few smokes to relieve the boredom. That an' takin' yer time to keep running your story over in yer head, of course, to make sure you've got it straight.'

'Silence in court!' Judge Neal banged his gavel on the table in front of him. 'We are here today to decide whether Dean Comyn, the accused, shot Mrs Effie Cambray on the night of 15 February 1886 at her homestead. How d'yer plead, Comyn?'

'Not guilty!' he said with as much confidence as he could muster. So far, things had not gone as well as Dean had hoped. A frantic search for Della, his alibi and the foundation of his defence case was still going on. Not only that but, as the sheriff suspected, the US Commissioner had ordered that the trial be held in Kansas where Mr Comyn was little known and where as a consequence, it would be easier to find an unbiased jury. Traditionally, in cattle country, the majority of the population would side with one of their own, which was why the courts had been finding it so difficult to bring a prosecution against fence cutters that sought passage for their herds across settlers' land. With the increase in the number of settlers across the west, such bias in favour of cattlemen was no longer guaranteed. Comyn signalled to his defence team to push for de-selection of potential jurors, based on his gut feel as to whether he thought they had the demeanour of a cowboy or a farmer.

Then, just as Sheriff McMaster, who was the key witness for the prosecution, was being called to the stand, a message was passed quickly to Comyn's defence attorney. It was an update from the attorney's evidence collection team on the whereabouts of Della Peveril. A check with the Wells Fargo office showed that she had left Ramestown on the morning after the murder, and although she had a ticket to the western end of the line, she had got off earlier and was planning to take a train north.

'So, what do you want us to do?' his attorney asked.

'Carry on lookin' fer now,' Comyn said angrily. 'I ain't changin' me story.'

'But if Miss Peveril can't be found, you have no alibi. This kind of witness search is very expensive, you know?'

'Well, I ain't payin' fer it if yer don't find her. Search the cattle towns, the mining towns. She's an entertainer, remember?' Dean Comyn retorted. 'In the meantime just discredit McMaster's evidence as much as you can.'

'So, allow me to summarise for the benefit of the jury. What you are saying, Sheriff McMaster, is that on the night of the shooting you were riding back to town through the snowstorm when you heard a shout followed by a gunshot as you passed the Cambray homestead. Unable to gain immediate access on horseback, because the Cambrays' perimeter fence was made of barbed wire, you dismounted. Leaving your horse under a tree, you then proceeded on foot. As you did so, you saw a man who looked like Dean Comyn leave the cabin in a hurry and disappear into the night. Is that correct?' the prosecutor asked.

'Yes, sir,' Sheriff McMaster replied.

'And what did you do then?'

'I had to follow the fence for some way until I found a gateway in it, enabling me access to the property,' McMaster continued. 'By then, Comyn had got away. I entered the house to find Mrs Cambray lying dead on the floor, with a bullet wound in her chest. She had a small pocket Derringer in her hand.'

'Had there been any other signs of physical violence, such as a struggle or damage to the property?'

'Not that I could see,' Sheriff McMaster answered.

'Thank you,' the prosecutor said. 'Members of the jury, the doctor who attended to Mrs Cambray's body and the local gunsmith have confirmed in sworn affidavits that, in their opinion, the bullet that killed Mrs Cambray was fired by the Derringer. Thank you, Sheriff. That is all for now.'

'Attorney for the defence, any questions?' Judge Neal enquired. Dean Comyn's attorney rose to his feet.

'Thank you, Judge,' he replied. 'Sheriff McMaster, the night in question, when you found Mrs Cambray's dead body . . . It was a cold night, wasn't it? A very cold night, in fact: you mentioned being out in a snowstorm. Is that correct?'

'Yes, sir,' the sheriff replied.

'So it is dark and it is snowing hard. That must have significantly reduced the visibility, mustn't it?'

'Yes, sir.'

'And you claim, in spite of this significantly reduced visibility, that the man you saw leaving the Cambray's place was the accused, Dean Comyn?'

'That's right, sir.'

'But how can you be so sure, especially in these conditions, that it was him?'

'I recognized him from his gait and his build, sir, not his facial features.'

The jury laughed.

'Silence!' the judge shouted, bringing his court to order. The defence attorney sat down knowing that the jury had not missed his point.

'Will Mr Dean Comyn take the stand?' Judge Neal demanded. Handcuffed, Dean was pushed by one of the court officials towards the stand. He looked at the man and snarled.

'Can you tell the court where you were at the time of the shooting, please, Mr Comyn?' the prosecutor asked.

'I was in town with my girlfriend, in her room at the hotel.'

'Della Peveril, that is, I presume?'

'Yep, that's right.'

'And will she testify before the court that you were with her?'

'She will when we find her,' Dean replied. There was sniggering from some members of the jury.

'What was your relationship with Mrs Cambray?'

'She was a neighbour. She and her husband were new to the area. Settlers. Her husband had gone line riding for the winter, so I offered to look in on her while he was away, see she was OK.'

'Very neighbourly, Mr Comyn.'

'I would say so, yes sir.'

'So that's how you would describe your relationship: you and Effie Cambray were just good neighbours?'

'Yes, sir.'

'Was there anything of a more intimate nature between you?'

'No, sir.'

'Would you have liked there to be?'

'Mrs Cambray was an attractive woman, but like I say, I already have a girlfriend.'

The prosecutor decided to try a different tack.

'Do you own a pair of gloves, Mr Comyn?'

'Yes, I do own a pair.'

'What colour are they?'

'They're black. Black leather.'

'Although you don't own a pair any more, do you, Mr Comyn?' Dean was taken aback. Where was this line of questioning leading? The prosecutor was passed an article by his clerk. 'Is this yours?' he asked, holding up a black leather glove.

'No,' Dean replied, trying not to sound nervous.

'Look inside it, please,' said the prosecutor, passing the glove to Dean. 'Can you see the initials 'DC' embossed inside?' Dean nodded. 'They're your initials, aren't they?'

'They are indeed,' Dean replied, thinking on his feet. 'And this is my glove. I wondered where it had got to. Where did you find it?

'It was found on the night Mrs Cambray died, in her parlour.' The prosecutor stared at Dean Comyn as the jury gasped.

'Maybe so,' he replied, 'but I lost that some time ago, long before the night of her death. Like I say, I used to visit her quite regularly. I must have dropped it on one of those previous occasions.' The prosecutor returned to his seat feeling a little deflated, while the defence had no further questions for Dean Comyn.

'Court adjourned 'til nine o' clock tomorrow morning!' the judge advised.

Dean Comyn slept better that night. All in all, things hadn't gone too badly on the first day of his trial. Not only had the prosecution failed to establish he was at Mrs Cambray's homestead at the time of her death but they had also failed to establish any motive. Della was a loose end, but if she didn't turn up he could still carry on maintaining that he was with her on the night Effie died. The prosecution had no categorical proof that he was at the Cambray homestead that particular evening.

As a consequence, he was surprised when he met his defence team for breakfast in his cell that they did not share his view. 'What's-a matter, boys?' Dean said in a jaunty voice. 'Why look so glum?'

'Listen, Dean,' his attorney said with a very serious look on his face. 'We have some good news and some bad news.'

'Go on,' Dean prompted. 'Get to the point.'

'The point is this. Thanks to our network of associates and the good offices of Wells Fargo, we found Della Peveril late yesterday. In Silver Mountain, to be precise. The bad news is that, as a result, she has sent us a wire witnessed by the local marshal there. She has informed us that she will not be attending the court as a witness because she says that the only time she saw you on the night in question was just for a few minutes, late in the evening, probably just after 10pm when you knocked on the door of her room.'

Dean Comyn's jaw dropped. Before he could say anything, his defence attorney started to explain that he had to pass this information onto the judge because this new evidence was potentially critical to the outcome of the case.

'The problem is, Comyn, you have lied to us – the team trying to defend you – and you have lied to the court,' the defence attorney pointed out, trying to control the anger in his voice. 'The prosecution won't let this go now, so you are going to have to come clean and tell the court exactly where you were at the time of Cambray's death.' The attorney got up to leave. 'The good news, if there is any good news, is that you've still got an hour before your trial resumes to work that out, and the reason why you didn't inform the court of this at the outset!' he added as a parting shot.

'So, Mr Comyn,' the prosecutor said with a wry smile, 'you

have had a change of heart and wish to tell us a different story as regards your whereabouts on the evening that Mrs Cambray died. Please go ahead.'

'I did visit Mrs Cambray on the evening in question,' Dean Comyn said bowing his head, as if in shame. The loud gasp of the occupants filled the courtroom with foreboding.

'And why didn't you tell us that earlier? Your girlfriend and alibi has left you. Were you hoping in the end that she couldn't be found or if she was, that she would still lie to this court for you?'

'No,' Comyn said raising his head. He looked the prosecutor directly in the eye. 'I am in a strange town, being tried by a jury that I don't know. You don't have sufficient evidence to prove that I fired the bullet that killed Mrs Cambray, in the same way that I don't have sufficient evidence either to prove that I didn't. I was scared that I might not get a fair trial. There's a lot of bad feelin' between settlers and cattlemen in these parts.'

'Are you tryin' to say that Sheriff McMaster didn't see you leave the Cambray homestead?'

'No, I am not tryin' to say that. If he says he thinks he saw me, then maybe he did. Maybe he didn't and mistook me for somebody else. Who knows?' Comyn shrugged his shoulders.

'Why, was there somebody else with you?'

'No, not while I was there. Just me and Mrs Cambray. Whether somebody else came after I wished her good evening and left, I don't know, but maybe somebody else did come. There are plenty of men who are the same build as me and walk the same way as I do. So, in that poor visibility it would be easy to mistake. Depends on what time it was, I guess.' The prosecutor realized that this smooth-talking man was beginning to lead him a dance around all the weaknesses in his case. Not only that, but he had taken a distinct disliking to this lowlife who had openly admitted lying to the court. He knew he needed to try a different approach so as not to have his professional reputation undermined.

'It would seem odd that, on such a stormy night, Mrs Cambray should have a string of visitors, would it not?'

'Objection, yer 'onour!' Comyn's attorney sprung to his feet, ready to take on the mantle.

Judge Neal looked up from his notes. 'Grounds?' he demanded to know.

'The line of questioning is irrelevant, yer 'onour. My learned friend is making unfounded and wild assumptions. Firstly, a second visitor does not constitute a string and could well have been someone lost and seeking shelter from the storm that later turned out to have dishonourable motives such as robbery, or even murder.

'Sustained!' Judge Neal called out.

'Did you and Mrs Cambray have any disagreement while you were with her that night?' the prosecutor asked out of desperation.

'No, sir,' Dean Comyn replied. 'We did not.'

'Members of the jury, you have heard both the cases for the prosecution and the defence,' Judge Neal said, addressing the twelve people before him. 'I am not here to tell you what to decide in this case, but I am going to give you some guidance in how to go about reaching a decision as to whether the accused, Dean Comyn, is guilty or innocent of the murder of Mrs Effie Cambray on the night of February 15th, so I demand that you listen closely.

'The prosecution's case in this trial has relied on what lawyers call circumstantial or indirect evidence as opposed to direct evidence. So, for example, if Sheriff McMaster had actually seen Dean Comyn shoot Mrs Cambray that would have been direct evidence. But he did not. What he saw and heard was a person who looked like Dean Comyn leaving the Cambray home and a raised voice suggesting an argument was taking place, followed by the sound of a gunshot, implying that that particular shot was the one that killed Effie Cambray.

'Circumstantial evidence is permissible in law, provided that the implication seems correct beyond reasonable doubt. The reasonable doubt test is often achieved by different pieces of indirect evidence corroborating each other, thus reinforcing the implication. The other piece of law frequently misunderstood by the layman is motive. If Mr Comyn did actually kill Mrs Cambray, what would have been his motive? As you heard from the evidence, no specific motive was either put forward or established by the prosecution. The fact that a motive was not suggested or proved does not prevent the jury returning a guilty verdict if the other evidence implies, beyond reasonable doubt, that the accused committed the crime.

'Now, two final matters of administration,' Judge Neal continued. 'You are no doubt aware that this state and other neighbouring states are made up of two main groups of people in terms of how you earn a living: cattlepeople and farmers. The dominant social group in terms of size and wealth in this area are the cattlepeople. In recent years this had made it difficult to select a jury without an inherent bias. We have tried to eliminate this possibility as far as is practical, by ensuring that the panel of jurors put forward for challenge and final selection by myself and the attorneys contains equal numbers of cattlemen, farmers and people from other walks of life.

'You may also have noticed that very few, if any of you, knew each other when you were selected to stand on this jury. And you'll recall that you were asked, as part of the selection process, whether any of you know or knew of the defendant. This is no accident and done to prevent small groups of people who not only know each other but had prior knowledge of the defendant's past and their behaviours from ganging up and influencing other members of the jury. You may indeed be very curious to know more about the defendant and tempted to make contact with the outside world to find out, but there is a risk that such information could well be hearsay and prejudice your judgment. Any attempt to try and do this would put you in trouble with the courts. Which is why, as you have probably also been wondering, this trial is being conducted in a different county from where the offence took place and in a small town off the beaten track, which has meant that you have had to stay overnight in the local hotel and not allowed outside without seeking prior permission. The US Commissioner specifically instructed that these procedures should be followed to help ensure that the defendant is tried fairly and free from the prejudice that has blighted many other trials.

'Finally, the court requires a unanimous verdict. I wish you well with your deliberations.'

'I ain't got time fer all this,' one old-timer moaned. 'I gotta start repairin' my property after the storms.'

'Me too,' somebody else chipped in. 'God knows how many cattle I've lost. Sat here on this damned jury while I'm probably losin' me livelihood. Don't get me wrong, my heart bleeds for that poor woman an' whatever it was exactly that happened to her, but whatever this court decides about the accused, it ain't gonna bring her back!'

'Damned court thinks justice is done if a life is taken for a life,' someone remarked, keen to get their beef off their chest. 'Dunno if I agree with that in this particular case. No true facts, all conjecture on both sides of the argument.'

'Listen!' a bank manager from the northwest intervened. 'This may not be as difficult as you might think. We need to put our emotions to one side for now and look at this systematically, then we can check how we feel about it.'

'Makes sense to me,' said a young man keen to get on with proceedings. 'I've got a pregnant wife back home and four kids. I don't wanna stay here any longer than needs be. None of us do. What do yer suggest, sir?' The clerk of court had thoughtfully left the jury with a large blackboard, easel and chalk at one end of the function room where they were assembled.

'Are you all happy that I chair proceedings? As a bank manger by profession, I am neutral as regards the settler versus cattleman issue raised by the judge.' The eleven other members of the jury voiced their approval. 'Come and gather round the blackboard.' As the jurors moved their chairs, the bank manager wrote three words on the blackboard.

'Guilty,' he said. 'Raise your hand if you think Dean Comyn is guilty of murder?' He looked round at the show of hands. 'OK,' he said, 'including me, "guilty" equals four,' and recorded the result on the blackboard. 'Right, how many people think he is innocent?' He checked the hands. 'OK, four,' he said writing the number on the board, 'so that leaves four not decided.'

'That means we are in the worst position possible if we are to reach a unanimous verdict!' someone shouted out. The bank manager raised his hand.

'Not necessarily,' he said. 'I want you to split into your three groups. "Not guilty" take your chairs and go and sit in that far corner over there. "Dunnos", go and sit in the opposite corner. "Guilty", stay here with me. Right, now listen up. "Dunnos" I want you to come up with a list containing the three items you find most convincing in terms of reaching a verdict and the three that you find the least convincing. "Not guilty", I want you to do something slightly different: I want you to come up with a list of the five pieces of evidence you found most convincing in terms of deciding the accused is not guilty. But I want you to score each of the five out of ten in terms of how convincing you found them. If the piece of evidence is a true direct fact, score it ten. If it is circumstantial and indirect, score it up to a maximum of seven. My group will do the same for the "guilty" verdicts. He took his watch from his waistcoat pocket. 'We'll check where we are in half an hour. Meanwhile, I'm just going to go and find the clerk of court and get some pencils and paper in case you want to write stuff down and more importantly, get some coffee for us all.'

The spokesman for the 'guilty' group stood up in front of the rest of the jury. 'We had just four pieces of evidence. The piece we found most compelling was the direct fact that the accused admitted to lying, thereby deliberately trying to mislead the court. We scored that at ten. In second place, we found his reason for lying weaker, especially given the rigour in the process this court has followed to ensure as fair a trial as possible. As a consequence, we gave that a seven.

'In equal third place, we thought Sheriff McMaster's identification of the man leaving the homestead as the accused and the glove being left behind on that occasion were more likely to be correct than less likely, so scored them as a six.'

The 'not guilty' group went next. Conversely, they scored the fact that Comyn had lied highly, on the grounds of being afraid that he wouldn't get a fair trial precisely because the judge had acknowledged that juror bias had been standing in the way of even-handed justice, thus giving Comyn's explanation credence. They also thought that Comyn's explanations about the glove and the sheriff mistaking someone else as him were plausible. The plausibility of alternative explanations as to what had happened on the night of the murder was the prime concern of the 'dunnos'.

After a short debate of the results, the bank manager asked the jurors to vote again. Most of them were surprised to find that those who thought Comyn guilty had doubled to eight, with the 'not guiltys' and the 'dunnos' both halving to two apiece. The crux of the issue boiled down to this: were the implications of each piece of evidence, when summed together, more or less likely to push the overall case beyond reasonable doubt?

'Ha ha,' the old-timer chuckled. 'That's very clever, mister. You got us to park our emotions and look at the issue systematically, then let 'em come back again but in a controlled way. An' it ain't even lunchtime yet!'

The bank manager then asked the two 'not guilty' to debate their case with half of the guilty group and the two 'dunnos' to do the same with the other half. Progress in the afternoon was a lot slower, but a check at seven o' clock showed the overall score had shifted to ten 'guilty', one 'not guilty' and one 'dunno'.

Maybe because the father-to-be was bringing a new life into the world, he still had problems with being complicit in the killing of someone on the grounds of 'beyond reasonable doubt' as opposed to 'beyond a shadow of a doubt'. At nine o'clock he moved across from the 'dunno' camp to the 'guilty' one, knowing that he was never going to persuade this group of people to reject an accepted point of law. Besides, he was anxious to get home as soon as possible where he had more important matters to attend to.

The remaining 'not guilty' supporter on the jury, the old-timer, accepted the logic argued by the majority but was concerned that his intuition still told him that this verdict was unsafe. By nine-fifteen, however, he had agreed to change it to 'guilty', on the basis that the intuition of one juror was not going to outweigh the logic supported by the eleven others in terms of argument, and perhaps neither should it. By nine-thirty that evening, Judge Neal had been advised of the jury's unanimous verdict.

CHAPTER 9

Dean Comyn lay on the bed in his cell. Three days to go. Three days before he was due to be hung for the murder of Effie Cambray. If Ramestown was becoming more and more like a ghost town, it certainly wouldn't in a few days time, as people would flock there from the surrounding environs. People loved a good hanging. The gruesome spectacle was almost therapy for them. Not only did it give them a chance to reflect on what could happen if they fell foul of the moral system – or that part of it to date that had been enshrined in law – but also allowed them to pat themselves on the back metaphorically that, thus far, they personally hadn't done so.

Ramestown jail was next to the railroad and Comyn had spent his first few days there putting together a case for an appeal in his mind, only to be informed when he shared it with his defence attorney that the US Commissioner had advised that an appeal would not be granted. To pass the time he then tried to imagine what it would be like to be dead, but soon gave up on that because it was just too difficult. Most of the time he spent just getting angry. Angry at those who he thought had done him down in life.

At one point, the Cambrays were at the top of his list. If he had never have met them then he wouldn't be in the position he currently found himself in. If that darned settler's wife hadn't been so attractive, he probably would never have offered to look in on her from time to time while her husband was away. However, in order to find a way to absolve himself of any blame, he began to think how he'd got to know the Cambrays in the first place, and that thought led him to his ex-boss, Holden Bauldry – that nasty, cowardly, ungrateful piece of work. Nasty because he had no compunction about intimidating others; cowardly because he always got other people to carry out his dirty work while keeping himself a safe distance; ungrateful because he wouldn't even give his loyal servant, Dean Comyn, a good character reference in court. In fact, he wasn't prepared to give the court any character reference at all. When Comyn's defence team approached Bauldry for the same, he denied ever knowing a Dean Comyn.

It wasn't long, however, before Holden Bauldry got knocked off the top spot on Dean's hit list. After a bit more thinking, he realized that there was only one person who could be top of the bill and that was that double-crossing bitch, Della Peveril. If a miracle were to happen and Dean managed to miss his hanging, he was going to hunt that woman down and tear her apart, bone by bone. His planned slaying of Holden Bauldry would look like a picnic compared with what he was going to do to her. In his mind, he ran through the story of how she had betrayed him again and how, as a consequence, he could justify taking his revenge on her.

'Sheriff McMaster,' a voice called from outside. The sheriff put his coffee down and got up out of his chair.

'Mack Cambray, good morning,' the sheriff said. 'I am very sorry for your loss,' he added politely, doffing his hat.

'Thanks, Sheriff,' Mack replied. 'That's what I've come

here to talk about.'

'OK, Mack. You'd better come inside. 'Fraid you'll have to let me take your gun. As you're no doubt aware, we've got the varmint who did it locked up inside an' I can't afford to take any chances.' Mack gave the sheriff his gun and they proceeded into his small office. As they sat down there was a loud clanging noise from Dean Comyn's cell. Sheriff McMaster exhaled his breath through gritted teeth and stood up.

'What d'yer want, Comyn?' he shouted out.

'Get me a glass of water,' Comyn shouted back. 'I'm thirsty!' The sheriff poured a glass and took it out to Comyn's cell.

'Up against the back wall, Comyn. You know the procedure.' Dean Comyn backed away from the cell door while the sheriff put the glass between the bars and down onto the floor.

'Begrudge a man on death row a glass of water, would yer?' Comyn snarled.

'No,' replied the sheriff. 'Just you!' McMaster returned to his office and shut the door. Dean Comyn could hear their muffled voices through the adjoining wall. Wondering what the hell Cambray wanted to talk to the sheriff about, Comyn emptied the glass of water through the bars of his cell window. He then placed the rim of the glass against the wall that divided his cell from the sheriff's office and held his ear against the base of the glass. He tried doing this in a number of different places until he found the spot where the vibrations created by the two men's conversation next door could be heard the clearest.

'I've only recently made it back from spending the winter out on the prairie to find that all this has gone on in my absence,' Mack Cambray began. 'I believe you were first on the scene on the night my Effie was shot?'

'That's correct,' Sheriff McMaster replied.

'You don't know if anything was stolen, do you?'

'It was not obvious that anything was. The place was in good order. There were no signs of a struggle or someone attempting to ransack the place. Why, is anything missing?' the sheriff asked.

'Yes, my wife's music box,' Mack Cambray replied. 'It was very special to her, a gift from her grandmother and probably worth a considerable sum of money. It was normally kept locked away and would only come out on the odd occasion when she wanted to listen to its sweet song.'

'I see,' Sheriff McMaster said thoughtfully. 'When you say worth a considerable sum of money . . . sufficient to warrant someone trying to steal it?'

'Yes, certainly.'

Dean Comyn was taken aback. That damned music box. He still didn't really know to this day why he took it as he ran out, leaving Effie Cambray dead on the ground. He remembered being in a panic at that time, almost a blind panic, when he saw the music box on the table behind the front door and just grabbed it. Various thoughts had flashed through his mind at the time. For example, taking the music box might make the unfortunate incident look like a burglary and thus more likely to move suspicion away from someone like him, who would have no interest in such an item, nor be aware of its value. Also, it might be a useful gift to bribe Della with to act as his alibi. In the end, he decided to pass the box to her and use her as his mule to keep it concealed by simply lying to her about how it had come into his possession. It was funny that she had not raised the issue with his attorneys when she decided to destroy his alibi. Maybe when she found out what it was, she sold it to keep herself out of the whorehouse where she rightfully belonged. He put the glass against the cell wall again and continued to eavesdrop.

'Did many people know of the existence of this music box?' Sheriff McMaster asked.

'No. It was not something that we boasted about – we were not that kind of couple. But wait, there were some. Two people in fact: Dean Comyn and Mose Alder, Holden Bauldry's nephew. Comyn didn't seem at all interested in the box but the boy was quite smitten with it.'

Sheriff McMaster went to speak but paused in order to fully process his thoughts first. 'OK,' he said finally. 'That's very useful, a very useful piece of new evidence. Needless to say, the investigations relating to this case have not unearthed the whereabouts of this music box, but its disappearance might have implications. I will need to talk to Judge Neal about it and I will get back to you. Thank you for dropping by.'

After Mack Cambray had departed from his office, Sheriff McMaster poured himself a strong black coffee and sat down to deliberate on what the implications of this new evidence could be. Comyn's trial had struggled to find a motive as to why Comyn had shot Effie Cambray but the boy, Mose Alder, had one – the music box. But then, the figure leaving the homestead looked so much like Dean Comyn. Yet, on the other hand, so did the boy: he was of a similar build and height to Comyn. The difference was that, as a teenager, Mose Alder didn't have the same coordination of movement as Dean Comyn. But one wouldn't necessarily be able to see that in heavy snow. Walking in deep snow doesn't give a person the same freedom of movement they would normally have. The restrictions make people's walking styles look a lot more similar.

Then, of course, what about Dean Comyn's glove being found in the homestead? How did that fit with the implications of Mack Cambray's new evidence? Sheriff McMaster took a slurp of his coffee before concluding that if Mose Alder was Effie Cambray's killer and had bluffed entry into her home in order to steal her music box, then the glove supported Dean Comyn's defence that he had been at the Cambray residence earlier that evening and that when he left, Effie Cambray had still been alive. This music box evidence had suddenly made the case a lot tighter. It would be difficult to prove though, because Holden Bauldry undoubtedly would provide his nephew with a cast iron alibi. Sheriff McMaster took a deep breath and rose out of his seat. He picked up his hat and walked up the street to the Wells Fargo office where he sent an urgent wire to Judge Neal.

After Mack Cambray had left the jailhouse, Dean Comyn had sat on his bed and also thought about the implications of the conversation he had just heard through the bottom of a glass. Unlike Sheriff McMaster, he chose to focus on those matters that he could influence directly.

'Just need to scare that halfwit Mose Alder into deliverin' me a gun,' he muttered to himself. With the sheriff out of the building, Dean paced his cell backwards and forwards as he started to concoct a plan. It centred around advising the boy that he may be wanted for questioning regarding the theft of a music box from Effie Cambray, and that if Mose wasn't prepared to help Dean break out of jail then Dean would tell the law that the boy had offered him the music box in return for a large sum of money. *Yep*, Dean thought to himself. *The kid was gullible enough to fall for that.* All that Dean needed to do now was to work out how to relay that message back to the kid. Also, unlike Sheriff McMaster, Dean Comyn was starting to find himself in an upbeat mood.

CHAPTER 10

Holden Bauldry stared out of the open second-floor window of the Ramestown Cattlemen's Association building at the growing numbers of people in the street below. Their constant babble, punctuated by the sound of regular hammer blows from the erection of a gallows at the bottom of Main Street, was a brief but welcome contrast to the sombre atmosphere that pervaded the upstairs room.

'Ironic, isn't it?' Holden remarked as he shut the window to cut down the noise.

'What's that?' Judd Rames asked while pouring them both a glass of whiskey.

'All these people comin' into Ramestown for the hanging tomorrow. The volume of people is reminiscent of the good old days when Ramestown was the place to be, but the hanging is symbolic of the town's death thanks to the demise of the cattle trail business.'

'Huh,' Judd responded. ' 'Fraid those "good old days" are over.'

'Why do'yer say that?' Holden enquired. 'They ain't over. Not yet. Jest gone away, for a bit. But they'll be back, mark my words,' he said, jabbing the air in front of him with his finger. 'People haven't suddenly got an aversion to beef; it's still a staple for them. Don't you agree?'

68

'For me, I must admit, all that has happened of late – the death of my son Judd junior, the "big die-up", which has resulted in the loss of large numbers of cattle and the subsequent bankruptcy of many cattlemen, the economic collapse of this town, and the reduction in size of the open range as more settlers come west – all mark the end of an era. One that we will never forget, mind you, and one that we will all learn from. But those sad events also mark the beginning of a new era. The nation still wants and expects us to do what we do for them, but we will just have to work out how to do it in a different way.'

'You got plans, then? You know how you're gonna do that?'

'Yes, I do. I've spoken about it with my line rider, Mack Cambray,' Judd advised. Holden Bauldry winced at the mention of that man's name. Although he had managed to keep his involvement between the Cambrays and his ex-employee, Dean Comyn, out of the public eye, his intuition told him that this situation was still a loose end.

'So, what did Cambray recommend yer do?'

'To go back to Texas and buy a ranch.'

'You're joking, ain'tcha? What, like the XIT and the Frying Pan ranches?'

'Well, I'd be joking about getting' somethin' that big. I couldn't afford to do that. But from the good years, I've got some money put by. I could afford to buy and fence several thousand acres. I was lucky. Some of my herd survived the winter.'

'You were,' Holden commented. 'I lost virtually all mine. I'm havin' to spend my savings startin' over. Couldn't afford to buy any land. Not that I want to: cattlemen still have rights to use the open range an' that's what I'm gonna continue to do. Still cowboys around who wanna do that type of work rather than spend their days fixin' fences.'

'Trouble is, Holden, the open range is shrinkin', not only in size but ease of access as more and more of it gets fenced off. All the time settlers are allowed to come west, claim their one hundred and sixty acres and settle on it. There's less and less free land for us to graze our cattle. We have some rights, sure, but settlers have got priority. The federal government would rather see the west populated with people than cattle. Besides, there are other advantages of fencin' land in Texas.'

'Oh, and what are they?' Holden asked.

'Well, first of all, when Texas became a state in '45 it managed to keep title to its land because its territory never belonged to the federal government prior to joinin' the Union. Consequently, it can sell or lease its land to whomever it wants to, which it does. Ultimately this means that I can buy as much land as I want, whereas around here I can only claim one hundred and sixty acres.'

'OK, I get that,' said Holden, 'but aroun' here you don't have to pay anything. Open range is still free. Why do you wanna pay out good money to have yer own land? We have ways and means of keeping the settlers at bay. Admittedly, they are not all strictly legal, but it works.'

'I wan' my own land cos I can fence it in. Fence it in with cheap but effective barbed wire,' Judd explained. 'An' you're now askin' yerself, "why do I wanna go the trouble of fencin' it all in an' havin' to maintain those fences", I bet?'

'Yeah, I am,' Holden admitted. 'You're ahead of me. Go on.'

'This is the interestin' bit. This is what Mack Cambray told me. He said that keepin' cattle fenced in means they can't wander so far, and thus grow fatter. They are less susceptible to bein' stolen by rustlers. There's a small fortune to be saved in not havin' to brand them as well. Think about the winter we've jest had. We can store feed for the cattle to see them through the winter and keep them safe from wolves and the like. Fencin' makes it easier to control breedin', ultimately improvin' the quality of the herd. At the end of the day it all adds up to a higher quality product, for which we can charge more. And, with railroads bein' built all over the place, there's no longer the need for the long trail drives to get the cattle to market.'

'OK, kind of sounds plausible,' Holden admitted reluctantly. 'But why should Cambray tell you all that? He's a line rider; he's doin' himself out of a job, ain't he?'

'Well, he was a line rider, but he helped me out last winter as a kind of favour, really. He wanted to become a farmer but he needed some extra cash. But I wasn't gonna let those reasons undermine the power of Mack Cambray's wisdom. He's a true frontier man. He's always lookin' ahead an' knows that there's certain types of change you can't stand in the way of or ignore. You've got to learn to adapt an' stay ahead of the game.'

'I can see you're serious,' said Holden.

'Sure am,' Judd confirmed. 'I'm already in negotiations to buy some land in Texas an' I've got my eye on some more.'

'If you'd have known this earlier, would you have gone ahead with Ramestown?'

'Probably not, but it's easy to be wise with hindsight. Besides, I made some money out of the town, as you must have. I didn't lose on it, although it took up a lot of my time. Of course, what I could have never have known when we started building Ramestown, as none of us could, was that we were gonna have a winter as devastatin' as the last one. An' that's what finally made up my mind to move back to Texas.

'Anyway, what you gonna do, Holden? There's little growth in the grass around here. The roots have been damaged by the winter snow and ice.'

'I know,' said Holden. 'I'm in the process of buyin' a new herd with the money I made from Ramestown. Smaller than before but it's all I can afford. Gonna head up north, Wyoming, Montana way, and try again. I love the freedom of the range and the trail. Besides, we're unlikely to have another winter like the last one.'

Dean Comyn sat in his cell, his head racing with his ideas. He'd given up contemplating his fate at the gallows tomorrow at midday. He'd spent too much of his time in this cell contemplating dying. There was no point to that. Better spend what were potentially his last few hours on contemplating living and escaping the gallows. There had been no change to his personal circumstances as a result of Mack Cambray's new 'evidence'. The only change Dean was aware of to his situation was when McMaster told him that his hanging was being put back from dawn to midday. This was to give the poorer folk in the surrounding area that wanted to watch him hang the chance to travel there and back in the same day. The hanging of Dean Comyn was going to be the big, spectacular finale in the story of Ramestown, the entertainment capital of the county once upon a time.

But Comyn was no longer angry about that. Midday gave him several more hours to develop and review his plan. He decided that once the kid came and passed the gun through his cell window, he would set fire to his straw mattress. As Sheriff McMaster burst into his cell to put the fire out and stop the star of the show from disappointing his public by meeting an early death, he would shoot McMaster. Timing was of the essence. The railroad had lain on a special train for the hanging, due to arrive at 11am. Once Dean had broken out of jail he planned to be on that train as it left town. He wondered at first if the sheriff must have thought it a bit odd that, over the last couple of days, his prisoner had kept asking him the time throughout the mid-morning period. But McMaster kept obliging by giving him the required information, so Dean thought the sheriff must have put it down to his prisoner being bored and that the mornings were dragging. In fact, Dean was attempting to calibrate the position of the sun against bars of his cell window, so that at quarter to eleven, on the day of his hanging, he could implement his breakout plan.

It would all depend, however, if the particular lowlife he had spoken to through his cell window were going to pass his message onto the boy, Mose Alder. So far, he'd had a lucky break in that he'd been able to brief the lowlife while McMaster had gone across to the Wells Fargo office to collect a wire.

Dean was surprised when the sheriff came back to the jailhouse and strode up to his cell door straight away. 'Listen up, Comyn!' McMaster boomed. Dean's jaw dropped. He thought the lowlife must have double-crossed him and informed the sheriff of the contents of his message.

'You're free to go, Comyn!' the sheriff said.

'What?' Dean shouted, hardly able to believe his ears.

'Says so here in this wire I've just received,' Sheriff McMaster explained. 'The legal people have reviewed your case. There's been new evidence. They have decided your conviction is unsafe.'

CHAPTER 11

After learning about the death of his wife following his return home, Mack Cambray put his energy into his work. Within a month, with some help from his neighbours, he had erected his windmill and was pumping water not only for his own homestead but others as well. His water business, as he called it, meant that he did not have to spend time farming his land as his neighbours provided him with food in return for his advice and help on how to find and tap sources of water.

This community spirit between groups of neighbours grew, and culminated within a few months in the establishment of the Ramestown District Settlers and Homesteaders' Association to look after their individual and joint interests, in much the same way as the cattlemen's associations did for the cattlemen. Mack was invited to be its first president, a post that he was keen to accept for a number of reasons. Although as a line rider he was used to his own company for long periods of time, he found that he was in greater need of social contact, especially in this grieving period, and working with people gave him focus. It also provided him with a network of people in the area and information about what was happening there. It was through this network that he had learnt that Holden Cambray had gone to Wyoming and Montana territories in search of open range, and that he had taken his nephew, Mose Alder, with him. A number of settlers explained to him that Holden Bauldry had ordered Dean Comyn to harass the Blake family into giving up their settlement and that Sheriff McMaster was unable to do anything about it without any solid evidence. Also, he had learnt from these sources that, once freed, Dean Comyn had been escorted out of town by a special posse for his own safety and taken to the railroad station in Kansas. There was a rumour going around that he was heading to Silver Mountain to find Della Peveril.

Mack Cambray turned this information over in his head frequently when he was alone in his cabin, and started to do so once again. Somehow he needed to get closure so that Effie's death would not appear in vain. Eventually, as he regained full control of his emotions and was able to give objective thought its head, he rationalised that his wife must have died in one of three ways: she either shot herself, or she was shot by accident – possibly in some sort of struggle – or she was murdered. Out of those three, he thought suicide the most unlikely. Many women had gone mad living in the harsh conditions of the west but Effie was made of stronger stuff than that and would not have been worn down by the harshness of some of the living conditions. She may, however, have shot herself to protect her honour, in which case she would have succeeded in her motive, but in that circumstance was far more likely to have shot her assailant. Of course, suicide may have been likely if there had been a number of assailants, but there had been no evidence of this in the same way as there had not been any evidence of a struggle.

This last fact suggested that Effie's shooting might have been some kind of accident brought about either directly by her own actions or whoever had been with her at the time.

Did the shouting that Sheriff McMaster said he heard immediately before the firing of the gun fit into that scenario? Possibly. Certainly, if it was a shout that had warned of an accident about to happen.

Then, of course, there was the most popular theory: that Effie was murdered. Lack of proven motive hadn't stopped Dean Comyn almost reaching the gallows on the grounds that he had committed the murder. That was until, almost unwittingly, Mack had discovered a potential motive in that his wife's beloved music box had gone missing. The music box, however, could have gone missing at any time and not be connected to Effie's death at all. Effie may have lent it to the boy to enjoy, for example. That would have been typical of her good nature. It would be very good to find it, establish what had happened to it and work from there.

But who could the murderer have been? If one ruled out the possibility, at least for the time being, of some unknown person being with Effie at the time that she died, then there were four identifiable people that could have been or maybe knew who was. Mack knew that he had to find these people, however long it took, and talk to them. He took a pad and paper out of the dresser and wrote down a brief personality profile alongside each of their names.

The first profile he drew up was Holden Bauldry. He had a reputation as a bully, but appeared to always keep a safe distance so that he could not be incriminated for such. For example, the case of the Blake family and also, when arrested for murder, his henchman Dean Comyn had received no support whatsoever from his boss. Bauldry had either been very clever and ruthless about covering his tracks, or not involved in Effie's death at all.

Next, he worked on Comyn's profile. Both he and Effie had been taken in by this man's charm only to find that Comyn at best was a liar and a scoundrel. Was he really that scared of not getting a fair trial that he had lied so blatantly? Regardless, he sounded like the type of character who might be out for revenge: a dangerous man who lived by the sword and no doubt would die by it. Mack knew he had to get to him before that happened. Dean Comyn undoubtedly knew a lot more than he was letting on but it would probably be very difficult to prise that information from him.

Then there was Mose Alder, the boy or kid as people still referred to him, even though he was nearly a man. Mose didn't seem the murdering type, although his lack of coordination and awkward manner would make him a potential suspect in an accident scenario. As regards being involved in a murder, a robbery, or any other crime for that matter, Uncle Holden would make sure that his nephew had a cast iron alibi. On the other hand, there was an honest streak still in the boy. He had not as yet got to casting off the innocence of youth. On his own, to whatever degree he may have been connected with Effie's death, he would probably offer an honest account.

Finally, Mack wrote the name of Della Peveril on his pad. A showgirl. From Mack's experience, showgirls could be hard-bitten on the outside – perhaps not surprising given the environments they often worked in – but often soft and warm on the inside. What was Della Peveril? Was she more the cynical, hard-bitten type? Mack didn't know her but he remembered that Effie thought that underneath that tempestuous, fun loving exterior there was a different persona germinating: one of compassion, honesty and principle, waiting for its turn to rise to the surface. Effie wanted to cultivate her as a friend. Did that cultivation occur? If so, what was Della's involvement in Effie's death? Had she collaborated somehow with her on-off boyfriend Dean Comyn, and decided to leave town and ditch him when things got hot? If she wasn't prepared to support Comyn's alibi that he was with her on the night of Effie's death, did she know where he actually was?

Mack started to feel pleased. After days of feeling confused about this whole episode, a plan of action was beginning to drop out of his analysis. The two people he might be able to glean information from most easily were Mose and Della. And with luck from what he might learn, it could become easier to trick the other two into offering up information they might otherwise be reluctant to share. One thing for certain was that time was of the essence. He needed to get to Della Peveril first before Dean Comyn did. Tomorrow, he would make the journey to Silver Mountain. .

'Well, what did they say?' Holden Bauldry's foreman asked.

'They said we can stay but we won't be able to participate in their roundups or use their corrals,' Holden replied.

'These local stockmen's associations can't prevent us using this range. They've got no legal right,' the foreman pointed out. 'Government policy says that the public domain is open to everyone equally for grazing purposes.'

'True. They know that. They are jest lettin' us know that we are not wanted, an' we ain't in a position to take 'em on, on their own turf,' Holden pointed out. 'They said the range up here has become too crowded. Too many people come up from the south lookin' for better grazing after the bad winter has severely damaged their traditional range.'

'So what we do, Unc?' Mose Alder asked Holden. 'I expect no one 'round here wants to sell their herd and the rights to their range that go with it?'

'Not at a price anyone can afford,' Holden replied. 'The loss of cattle from the blizzards is gonna push beef prices through the ceiling. No, we're jest gonna have to push on to Montana Territory an' hope we have better luck there!'

*

Montana Territory turned out to be not much better than Wyoming in terms of overcrowding. Holden Bauldry's old nemesis – settlers' barbed wire – was very much in evidence, forcing newcomers to graze at higher altitudes where the pasture was of poor quality. Not only that but the spring weather, which had been particularly dry in Montana, had turned into a severe summer drought. What little pasture that had come through after the winter started to die off. Temperatures reached over a hundred degrees and many water sources dried up. The cattle looked thin and weakened.

'Guess this heat is to make up for last winter,' Holden remarked, mopping his brow.

'Let's hope it's that way 'round and this hot weather's not a precursor of another bad winter,' Mose said with a hint of pessimism in his voice.

'Very unlikely to get two winters that bad together,' Holden suggested. 'Folk ain't expectin' it. Drift fences are still standin' so no one I know, not even Judd Rames, is reconsiderin' hirin' line riders.' But his nephew's comment spooked him.

CHAPTER 12

There were two types of theatre in Silver Mountain. There were those that could be placed under the general heading of badlands – located among the various saloons, bordellos and dance halls of the infamous red light district – and there were a few, like the Globe Opera House, that came under the category of 'respectable entertainment houses', where respectable ladies could go together, unaccompanied by their men-folk. The Globe was built as a tribute to the great bard, William Shakespeare, and productions of his plays were shown there frequently, along with popular operas such as Gilbert and Sullivan.

At the other end of the scale was the Garland. A purpose-built theatre with curtained boxes down the sidewalls and a long bar at the front of the auditorium, this establishment catered for popular tastes, including song and dance, comedy and burlesque. The showgirls who appeared there were encouraged to drink with the punters in the bar area after the shows for more wages. Those who were really short of cash could earn even more money by drinking in private with clients in the boxes behind the closed curtains. Such activity was not to every girl's liking, in which case they basically had three strategies: either just put up with this 'occupational hazard', which many did, or run away and risk being blacklisted from other establishments in the town, which some did, or, unable to cope with the shame and disgrace, just shoot themselves, which a desperate few did.

Silver Mountain, a very successful mining town, had a population of several thousand people. Dean Comyn realized that that was why Della Peverill had come here. It was a good place to hide amongst the crowd. On arrival he had visited the hotel where, thanks to Wells Fargo's record keeping, her bags had originally been taken, thus resulting in his defence attorney's discovery of her whereabouts. Of course, he found that not only had she checked out days ago but had not left any forwarding address either.

He decided to have a drink in the hotel bar and start making plans. He scratched his newly grown beard while he sipped a whiskey. Growing a beard was the only real preparation he'd made for this trip. He realized that it would give him an advantage when he eventually caught up with Della, since she was less likely to recognize who he was immediately. Thus far, however, it had been the energy from his anger that had propelled him along. Now he knew he needed to switch over to brainpower and deploy cunning and stealth.

One assumption that he felt he could base his deliberations on safely was that Della Peverill would be holed up in the badlands district of the town. No doubt short of money, she would have to work, and the way that she enjoyed doing that successfully, as far as Dean was concerned, was by entertaining the lascivious hordes of local riff-raff in one of those low-end theatres or saloons. As he took out his money to pay for another drink, Dean suddenly realized that he was in a similar position himself and getting short of funds. He only had a little cash left and needed to lay his hands on some more quickly, not only to meet his living expenses but also to finance his search for Della in terms of, for example, payments for information. It wasn't the first time he'd hit a town with little in his pockets and no doubt wouldn't be the last, so he knew what he had to do. A booming mining town like Silver Mountain was a particularly attractive proposition as it was awash with cash and people willing to spend it in order to get a slice of the action, whether it was buying a claim, drink, women or other pleasures.

Although he enjoyed a game of cards, Comyn was not a professional gambler, but he had known a few in his time and had learnt a few things about what made them tick. For example, unlike Dean Comyn, the professional gamblers were not bad losers. Being cheated riled them but not losing. When they lost their last dollar on the turn of the card they'd calmly borrow some money from the house and play again, on the basis that they can't lose forever. Their credit would be good however, unlike Dean's as the new boy in town. But he had learnt to adapt the professional's principles to his own situation. If he couldn't borrow money from the house, Dean Comyn realized that he might be able to borrow it from the other gamblers he would be playing with in a private game. All he needed now was some official-looking document that he could offer as collateral to underwrite any loan he was able to extract from the other players. So, refraining from having another drink, Dean headed for the local claims office where he hoped to spend a fruitful afternoon.

When Mack Cambray arrived in the badlands of Silver Mountain he realized that the task of finding Della Peveril wasn't going to be easy. The kinds of people who worked in, and were regular patrons of the entertainment provided there didn't start appearing on the streets until early evening, and by mid evening many of them were no longer sober. The odds of finding her through asking someone on the off chance if they knew of her whereabouts were extremely slim. Besides, she wasn't stupid and, knowing that now Comyn was free and would be likely to come after her, she had probably changed her name. It would mean a tour of the saloons and shows to see if he could recognize her. At least it should be just as difficult for Comyn to find her, Mack reasoned, and that the person who pursued the task more systematically was likely to get to her first. In that sense, Mack felt he had the advantage. All he had to do now was keep his eyes peeled.

'Godammit!' Dean Comyn muttered under his breath. He had finished his business at the claims office and was now in the badlands district of town looking for a game of cards to fund his search of the entertainment establishments for Della. He glanced at the man who was walking towards him and seemed to be staring straight at him. 'It's Mack Cambray,' Dean said to himself. He was tempted to go for his gun but that would just create too much attention. *Cambray's an honest, law-abiding man*, he told himself. *Won't wanna shoot a free man.* Caught in the middle of the pavement and hemmed in by the crowds, he had nowhere else to go except to keep walking. Dean averted his gaze down to his feet. Mack Cambray passed him with no apparent sign of recognition. Dean awaited a tap on his shoulder from behind, but none came.

'Phew,' he muttered mopping his brow as he dived into a saloon and sat down at the bar. *Well*, Comyn, he thought to himself, *yer luck still's runnin' for yer. The beard must've fooled him. Wonder if me luck will extend to winnin' some money at that card game over there?* He walked over to the table.

'Wanna play poker, cowboy?' said one of the three men at the table. Judging from their dapper style of dress, they looked like professional gamblers.

'Don't mind if I do,' Dean Comyn replied. He wasn't put

off by the fact that he was competing against three professionals. Although the ones that he knew would claim that skill was the dominant factor over luck in poker, Dean's personal experience had taught him that a bit of luck and a bit of skill could still turn the tables. He looked up at the waiter by his side, 'Bottle o' whiskey, please,' he said.

Although not particularly a fan of song and dance entertainment, Mack Cambray thought that the quality of the show he had just witnessed at the Garland was below the standard of the few he had experienced in Ramestown and the type that Della Peveril might have appeared in. Still, he decided to stay and have a drink after the show with the female members of the cast in the auditorium bar.

'What d'yer say her name was, mister?' a chorus girl, who had sidled up to him, asked.

'Della Peveril,' Mack replied.

'Describe her to me, mister,' the woman demanded. Mack did as he was asked. 'Ah,' the chorus girl acknowledged. 'I know her. If yer go in one of the boxes with me, I'll include what I know for free. Otherwise, it'll cost yer two dollars.'

'No offence, ma'am,' Mack said, 'but I'd rather give you the two dollars.'

'Up to you, mister,' the chorus girl replied. 'No skin off my nose. The woman yer lookin' for did one show. She was a pretty good singer but got the sack 'cos she refused to go behind the curtain with any of the punters afterwards. Fancied 'erself as an actress. Too stuck up for my likin'. An' her name ain't Della Peveril, either, so she's a liar as well.'

'What name does she go by then?' Mack asked.

'Sallie Jane Attwood,' the chorus girl answered.

'Do you know where she went?'

'Yer askin' a lot of questions for two dollars, mister.' Mack put another dollar in her palm. 'Thanks. I dunno for sure but if she's followin' her career aspirations, like all us showgirls try to do, I'd suggest you try the Globe.'

'Yer damned well cleared me out, boys!' Dean Comyn exclaimed. The other three card players looked at him unemotionally. 'I was beatin' you all for a while.'

'In the end, you lost cos you played too many wrong cards,' one of the professionals said. The second player just shrugged his shoulders and the third said nothing.

'In the end, I lost 'cos I'm not good at holdin' me liquor,' Dean lied. None of the three professionals around the table with him drank, at least not while playing. One of them glanced at the whiskey bottle; it was still three quarters full.

'Yer wanna loan? Is that what yer askin' for, mister, so that you can carry on playin'?

'That would be mighty good of yer, if yer can see yer way clear,' Dean replied. 'I've got assets.'

'Let's see 'em then,' the professional said, tempted by the ease with which money could be taken from a man he considered to be drunk. Dean passed him the note of sale. The man read out its contents to his two colleagues:

'*I, Grover Hampton, having received $500 from the agents of Mr D. Comyn hereby on this day, the 1st September 1886, pass the title of my mine at Hampton Creek, Silver Mountain to Mr D. Comyn.*

Signed: G Hampton (Vendor)
D. Comyn (Purchaser)'

'You Comyn, then?' one of the other two men asked.

'Yep,' Dean replied. 'It's a good stock to have shares in.

Been some good early finds of silver there; verified as well.'

'We know,' said the third man. 'We know Hampton.' The other gamblers watched Dean's face. There was no nervous reaction. 'What's he look like, this Hampton?' Dean was annoyed that they were testing him to check that he wasn't trying to scam them.

'Thought you said you knew 'im?' Dean retaliated, feeling slightly irritated.

'We do,' said the man who read out the note of sale. 'We just wanna check if you do.'

'He's tall, bald and has a moustache,' Dean replied. It had been easy to get that information out of the claims clerk when Dean showed an interest in the mine, which was advertised on the 'Claims for Sale' board in the clerk's office.

'Didn't know Grover was sellin' it,' the second gambler remarked. 'Ain't askin' much for it, given that the last time I spoke to him he reckoned it was gonna be the most productive mine in his portfolio.'

'He always says that,' the third one pointed out. 'Sales patter. Otherwise, he's as straight as the next man. Makes easier money from procurin' new sites an' buyin' and sellin' 'em than diggin' out the minerals.'

'Hampton does alright for himself,' the second gambler said. 'The document's got the claims office authorisation stamp on the bottom of it an' it looks like Grover's signature.' Not only had it been easy for Dean to distract the claims clerk so that he could stamp a blank sheet of paper but it had also been easy to forge Hampton's signature from the notice for sale.

'The rest of it sure don't look like Grover's writin',' the first gambler said.

'The clerk wrote it out for us both,' Dean responded. He paused so as not to appear too anxious to close the sale quickly. There was silence. 'So, gentleman, I am offering you shares in my new enterprise at the price of 75 cents for every $1 share. What d'yer say?' The three men conferred.

'50 cents for every $1 share,' one of them said.

'Gentlemen, you drive a hard bargain, but I accept your counter-offer,' Dean replied.

'So how much stake money do yer wan' us to give yer?'

'I'll take $50 in hard cash, please, which gives you a hundred shares and twenty per cent ownership,' Dean replied. 'Waiter,' he called out. 'Three more glasses and another bottle of whiskey please!' The three professional gamblers looked at Dean cautiously.

'Why, gentlemen?' Dean said in polite admonishment. 'This is no longer a game between strangers! This is a game between friends! Here's to our new enterprise!' he exclaimed, raising his glass. The others began to open up a little and follow his lead.

Mack Cambray stood outside the Globe Theatre perusing the notices and the forthcoming events announcements. There was no sign of Della Peveril. Then again, this publicity only mentioned the headline performers, and maybe she wasn't ready for that level. This week, Shakespeare's 'As You Like It' was being performed and tonight's performance was already sold out. He went inside and looked at the programme printed especially for this play. And there, after the headliners and the heading cast, he found the name Sallie Jane Attwood. He bought himself a ticket for the next evening's performance in the front row of the circle, where he thought he would have the best uninterrupted view and be able to determine if Miss Sallie Jane Attwood was really Miss Della Peveril.

Throughout the evening, the stakes continued to be raised. As a consequence, two hours after the first toast, Dean

Cambray sold the remaining shares in his mine to the professional gamblers who were only too pleased to oblige. After all, they had just bought a mine with a sales price of $500 for $250, which they could either keep and earn dividends from or, no doubt, sell for a profit. As professionals, they knew that they could easily take this sucker for everything he owned. In good spirits at the thought of being on such an easy ride, they had, however, committed the cardinal professional sin of drinking while playing cards. They weren't drunk, far from it, but neither were they fully sober. They were at that slightly merry stage, where self-confidence has increased but at the expense of self-awareness. At that stage, they didn't notice Dean Comyn occasionally stack the deck when it was his turn to deal, or deal off the bottom. They also didn't notice that, when he put his hands beneath the table to get out some more stake money from his jacket, he would empty his whiskey glass onto the floor before making a big display of supposedly downing his glass in one and being ready for a top up.

The drunker his opponents became, the more Dean won. By the end of the evening he had turned the $250 stake money he had 'bought' from the professional gamblers into $500 hard cash in his pocket.

'Well, I guess that makes us quits, gentlemen,' Dean said as he got up to leave. 'Better luck with the mine than you had with the cards tonight.'

'You cheated on us, mister!' the angry sporting man spat the words out in disgust.

'If yer really think that's true,' Dean retorted, picking up his hat off the table and revealing his six-shooter, 'yer should have challenged me at the time. Good evenin', gents, and thanks for the company.'

By two o'clock the next morning, Dean Comyn was a little drunk himself. He felt he had deserved a small celebration. Back in funds, he had enjoyed a pleasant drink in the company of one of the showgirls in a box at the Garland Theatre. An obliging woman, she had informed him of the likely whereabouts of Sallie Jane Attwood, alias of Della Peveril.

CHAPTER 13

Fortunately for Mack, the lady sat next to him in the circle had a pair of opera glasses that, after he had introduced himself as a friend of the actress playing Celia, Sallie Jane Attwood, she was happy to share with him during the performance. Mack was unfamiliar with the works of Shakespeare but, although he had trouble following some of the language, he was quite taken in by the spectacle.

When Celia made her entrance in the second scene of Act One, Mack asked to borrow the opera glasses. He focused on Celia's face. Although heavily made up, there was no mistaking that it was the face of Della Peveril. 'Thank you,' he replied, handing the glasses back to his neighbour.

Dean Comyn had managed to buy a cancellation in the front row. Also unfamiliar with the works of Shakespeare, he soon realized that this was not his personal choice of entertainment. Overlooking the programme of the gentleman next to him, he could see that Della was playing a person called Celia. Dean nudged the gentleman and asked him to let him know when the character Celia came on stage. In Act One, Scene Two, the gentleman nudged Dean back.

It was during the interval that Sallie Jane Attwood was supposedly taken ill. She had peeped through the curtain at the audience only to confirm her worst nightmare. Sat before her in the front row, she spotted Dean Comyn. He may have had a beard but she could recognize those ice blue eyes anywhere. After all, she'd stared into them often enough.

'I've suddenly come over very poorly,' she said to the stage manager.

'I thought you'd seen a ghost out in the audience,' the stage manager remarked.

'I must return to my rooms, take my medication and lie down,' she explained.

'Don't worry, Miss Attwood,' the stage manager replied. 'You go. I'll prepare your understudy. We'll be all right here, trust me,' he reassured her.

Back at her rooms, Della flung her possessions into her bags and dragged them down the stairs. If she hurried, she could make the overnight train to Texas. Outside she found a Chinese man pulling an empty cart. He looked shocked as she flung her bags into the back of his cart and demanded he take them to the station. She offered him a dollar and his expression changed to one of gratitude.

For someone who thought he was going to fall asleep through this performance of 'As You Like It', Dean Comyn surprised himself as to how alert he actually was. As soon as the understudy walked on the stage, playing the role of Celia, Dean knew it wasn't Della. Had she recognized him from the stage and disappeared? He got up from his seat and made for one of the exits. Instinctively he thought she might have left the theatre. He exited by a side door and found himself in a small alley at the side of the theatre. He hurried down to where the alleyway joined the main street and there in the distance, he could see Della hurrying along and signalling to a Chinese man who was pulling a cart behind him, to keep up.

'I don't think your friend is still playing the role of Celia,' the lady next to Mack whispered in his ear as she offered him the opera glasses. He raised them to his eyes and took them down again immediately and passed them back.

'You're right,' he said. 'Something must have happened. I must go.' Downstairs, in the corridor, he spoke to one of the attendants.

'I'm afraid Miss Attwood has been taken ill, sir. She has already left the theatre.'

Mack stumbled out of the exit door into a dimly lit alleyway. Down the end, in the shadows, he could see a man about to leave the alleyway looking back over his shoulder. As the man started to run, a whip caught him around his knee and he fell to the ground. It was difficult to see exactly what was going on but a number of men appeared suddenly out of the darkness and one of them kicked the fallen man in the chest. Mack took out his gun and hurried along, keeping to the shadows so as not to be seen.

'We've spoken with Grover Hampton an' he never sold his mine to you.' The speaker kicked the man again in the chest. 'You owe us; you fraudulently took from us.'

'I ain't got it,' the man on the ground groaned. 'Can't get it until next week.'

'Be a thousand dollars by then, mister. Interest.' This time he kicked his victim in the face. Mack fired two shots in the air and then one just over the head of the man leading the assault. To his surprise there was no return of fire, with the gang deciding to cut and run.

Mack walked up to the man lying on the ground, whose face was covered in blood. 'I'll get you some help,' Mack said, kneeling down over the man.

'Thanks,' the man muttered. Just before his eyes closed and he lost consciousness, Dean Comyn recognized his saviour as Mack Cambray.

CHAPTER 14

If the winter storms of 1885-6 were bad, January and February of 1887 were no better. Following the extreme summer drought of '86, temperatures dropped to thirty degrees below and blizzards raged across the plains from Montana in the north to Texas in the south. Many cattle died of thirst or exposure, while predators like wolves attacked others. Some lost their hoofs to frostbite while others lost limbs on shards of ice as they fell through the ice sheets that covered their watering holes. Others died against the drift fences that had still been left standing after the previous winter, crushed by the weight of their own number.

Like many cattlemen, Holden Bauldry lost his entire herd that winter in Montana. Completely wiped out. But unlike many of them, spooked by his nephew's comment about the extreme summer being a precursor of another bad winter, Holden Bauldry had travelled periodically back and forward to the Ramestown district the previous autumn, each time with a different one of his men.

As an insurance policy against being squeezed off his old range on his eventual return south, he made three homestead claims: one in the northwest corner of his old range, one in the southwest corner and one in the southeast. To legitimise the claims each one was made in a different name, albeit all three claimants worked for Holden Bauldry. He decided to redefine the northeast corner by taking on some railroad plots. In spite of taking out a large loan secured against his ranch house, buying this land in the northeast corner was too expensive, so he decided to lease it instead. There were a number of advantages to leasing plots from the railroads, who were originally granted the land along the rail corridors by the government as a subsidy to help pay for the roads' construction.

First, the railroad terms were often favourable, with some allowing payment by ranchers over a ten-year period paid in annual instalments with interest. This enabled the land to be leased at a very reasonable rent. Second, the government implemented its railroad land grant system on a checker-board basis. Thus, the Public Land Survey divided the grant into 640-acre numbered sections whereby every other section was retained by the government as public land (the even-numbered sections), which they had hoped to sell set-tlers, but eventually gave much of it away to the financially poor settlers under the Homestead Act. By fencing in the outside boundaries of the sections he had purchased or leased (the odd-numbered sections), a rancher could effec-tively gain the use of the public section in between for free, an opportunity that had not escaped the notice of Holden Bauldry. The third and perhaps most important advantage was that by acquiring the northeast section in this way, he had cheap access to water from a creek that flowed across that part of the range.

Having acquired well over a hundred thousand acres of ranch land from his old range and the railroad plots, Holden's next move was to hire cowboys to start building fences and thus join all the acquisitions he'd made on his old range together, thereby fencing in the land between them as well. Although execution of this latter move would violate the 1885 Act of Congress forbidding construction and maintenance of enclosures on public lands, Holden figured that the Act would be difficult to enforce, given the difficulties of record keeping and fact finding across such wide spaces. Besides, if it came to it, he could also argue that he had rights to the land through prior possession, supported by legal precedent.

Dean Comyn went to ground for a few months following his almost fatal beating in Silver Mountain. He was nursed for a while by nuns at a Catholic mission but, as soon as he was better, all the good intent he had shared with his carers throughout his stay to lead a more righteous life evaporated as the old motivations took hold once more: those of making money, and avenging the injustices foisted upon him by Della Peveril and Holden Bauldry.

Throughout the autumn months of 1886, Dean Comyn had travelled around mining towns of the northwest, operating the gambling scam he had played in Silver Mountain. He had used the period of mediation and reflection, enforced on him by the nuns, to consider how he could improve the scam, and one of the conclusions he reached was that in any one town, play the scam just once only and then take the money and run.

Unfortunately, the opportunity to make a sustainable living this way was limited by the number of mining towns. Dean had considered, as he rode back south to his old stamping ground, returning to each of the towns after a respectable passage of time and playing the scam again, but the sight of a church spire in the distance and its graveyard on the hillside had brought back the horrors of what could happen if things went wrong and there were no good Samaritan to rescue him.

With Ramestown rapidly becoming a ghost town, Dean

spent the winter in Kansas where he lived comfortably, playing the gambling halls more for pleasure than the need to gain an income. As spring broke and the snows receded, he ventured west onto the prairies. On arrival, he found that things had changed significantly. Although there was still open range, the volume had decreased as more and more settlers had arrived and strung up more and more barbed wire to protect their claims. The war he had fought on behalf of Holden Bauldry to stop their influx by intimidation, and cutting their fences to gain passage across their land appeared to have been lost. Even the cattlemen were fencing in land now. A reaction to two bad winters was sounding the death knell for the open range by its former fiercest advocates.

As he travelled around talking to people, Dean learnt that a new fence-cutting war was starting to break out. Whereas in the past it had been the big cattlemen cutting the settlers' fences, this time the settlers were siding with the small cattlemen, those with small herds who couldn't afford to buy their own land, and cutting illegal fencing erected by the big cattlemen on public land. The whole situation was a recipe for chaos with new settlers arriving to find that land they had hoped to claim had been taken illegally by big cattlemen.

As far as Dean Comyn was concerned, wherever there was chaos there was opportunity. He just had to sharpen his focus and find it. Was it on one side or the other, or did it lay elsewhere? He didn't have to sharpen his focus much. The opportunity was there right before his eyes. With most people now keeping their livestock in enclosures, they had stopped branding them, and that's where Dean Comyn's next career move lay: rustling. It was far easier to steal unbranded livestock and get away with it than branded livestock. Not only that, but if he stole settlers' livestock or small cattlemen's livestock, the big cattlemen would get the blame, and when he stole cattle from the big boys, the settlers and the small cattlemen would get the blame!

Mack Cambray's quest, to find the people who might be able to help him uncover the truth about what really happened the night his wife had died from a single bullet wound, had come to a halt. Della and Comyn had disappeared, while Mose and Bauldry, although local, lived in seclusion, denying Mack the degree of closure he would have liked. Generally, he was able to immerse himself in his work. However, there were times when his thoughts drifted to Effie and whether she died in a state of absolute fear or extreme pain. He still felt that if she were unable to share that knowledge with someone who cared about her, then her soul would struggle to rest in peace. It was the start of spring and approaching the anniversary of her funeral. They had held off burying her at the time and preserved her body, awaiting the melting of the ground frost, the outcome of the murder trial and Mack's return. There were still a few weeks to go before he would journey to her grave the other side of Ramestown and commemorate the first anniversary of her being laid to rest and he sensed that they might be a difficult few weeks.

As settlement of the area increased, so Mack's water business continued to grow, as did membership of the Ramestown and District Settlers and Homesteaders' Association. The ongoing success of his water business had allowed him to employ labour to farm and improve his own homestead. For the gift of this knowledge, he would always be eternally grateful to his father, who saw it as a mission in life that his son should know how to live off the land, whatever obstacles he might encounter. For the experience gained from the practical application of this knowledge, he thanked his time spent on the range as a line rider. To help others acquire the same wisdom gave Mack's life a meaningful purpose. This had started to become so important to him that he was contemplating resigning from his presidency of the association to devote more time to this cause.

Della Peveril always had a lot of time for Judd Rames. He was like her kind surrogate uncle. She admired him as a man and for his achievements, but most of all she respected his advice and wise counsel. On a number of occasions over the years she had sought his mentoring to help her through a difficult situation. Which was why, when she arrived in Texas on that overnight train from Silver Mountain, one of the first things she did was to journey out to his ranch.

On her overnight journey south, she had used the time to reflect less on her situation and more on herself. How she had grown, where she had been and what she had become. Silver Mountain had been a wake-up call, a transitioning period.

Her experiences there, both good and bad, had enabled her to take an objective view of her life. She began to see in her desire to be herself, how the sometimes tempestuous and impulsive side of her nature could deteriorate into self-indulgence if unchecked. Although her spell at the Globe had been brief, in terms of discovering her own significance and setting her free, it had been a revelation to her. She had relayed these thoughts to Judd Rames when she met up with him on his ranch.

'My dear Della,' he said. 'It sounds like, in a professional sense at least, you are ready to bring more stability to your life and seek your fulfilment elsewhere, in this case, perhaps, by passing on your knowledge to others. Your newfound wisdom has enabled you to come of age, so to speak. It is good. It doesn't happen to all of us, but you are fortunate if it happens to you. It happened to me with taking on this ranch and giving up the open range. I have learnt more about life from this experience than I ever did from establishing Ramestown.'

'Thank you for your encouragement, Judd,' Della said, smiling. 'I am looking to hire a room in one of the surrounding towns where I can give drama and music classes.'

'Might be able to go one better than that,' Judd exclaimed.

'Oh?' Della said, looking surprised.

'The local school doesn't currently have a teacher and is being run by parents at the moment, but that's not sustainable. It would mean teaching kids the three Rs, not just drama, but the building has accommodation as well and the money is good. Would you be interested?'

'Sure would,' Della replied.

Mack Cambray had almost finished writing out his resignation from his presidency of the Ramestown and District Settlers and Homesteaders' Association when a loud banging on his door interrupted him. He got up to answer it.

'Mr Cambray! Mr Cambray! My husband's been shot in the leg. They're gettin' up a posse an' wan' your approval to go after Bauldry!'

'You'd better come in, Mrs Spencer.' Mack stood aside as the settler's wife bustled past him into his ranch house. 'Take a seat and tell me what happened.'

'My Jake had decided to take our sheep down onto the public land early this mornin' cos it's better grazin' than we've got, what with the lambin' an' all that. He went down by the railroad where Bauldry has effectively fenced in sections of the adjacent public land. Although those fences are actually erected on Bauldry's land, they're so close that there's not wide enough access at the corner to get from one public section to the next. Anyways, my Jake was contemplating cuttin' the fence to gain rightful access when he was fired on by a couple of masked men. Put a bullet in his leg. Told 'im that was a warnin' not to stray off his own land.'

'How's Jake now?' Mack asked.

'Oh, he's recoverin',' Mrs Spencer relied. 'Doc came an' removed the bullet. What about the posse? Shall I tell 'em you've authorized it?

'I can't authorize it, I'm afraid. I'm not a law enforcement official,' Mack explained.

'But my Jake didn't do no wrong, did 'e? He only thought about cuttin' the fence. He didn't actually do it.'

'No, Mrs Spencer. Jake didn't do anythin' wrong,' Mack reassured her, 'and I'm pretty certain the courts would find against Bauldry. Even though the fences are erected on his land, they would be considered a nuisance as they are preventing access to the public domain. I'd better ride back with you and talk to your posse before they turn into vigilantes. I'll go get my horse.' On his way out, Mack Cambray grabbed his guns, tore up his resignation letter and threw the pieces in the stove.

Della Peveril was really enjoying her new job. She now felt fully equipped to be the mistress of her own destiny without any encumbrance. Her school building was suitably equipped and, for the first time in several years, she was able to live in more than just one room. Work was still a pleasure rather than a chore, just as it was when she used to perform on the stage.

As the evening light began to fade, she was starting to feel ready to turn in, but thought she might hunt out her book of Shakespeare's sonnets and read it in bed for a while. She believed that she had already unpacked it, and scoured the

bookcase for the title, but to no avail. Then she wondered if ·
was still in her travelling bags, as it was only a small book and
may have easily fallen to the bottom.

Della pulled out the bags from under the bed. They had
been her travelling companions for several years. Their contents had never been emptied fully for quite a while as she
had literally lived out of them on many an occasion, filling
their seemingly infinite dark spaces slowly with various bits
and pieces she had acquired on the way. Bits and pieces that
seemed appropriate to have at the time but subsequently
had not been used and forgotten about. As she rummaged
around in the bottom of the bags, her hand settled on a
small package.

'What's this?' she muttered as she pulled the object out of
the bag and into the light where she could inspect it. She
recognized the black tissue wrapping. 'My god!' she said out
loud as her memory recalled how she had acquired the
article. 'Dean Comyn gave this to me on the night that poor
Effie Cambray was murdered. Asked me to look after it,' she
mumbled to herself. She felt the adrenaline course through
her veins as she unwrapped the parcel to reveal a small
wooden music box. She opened the lid and wound it up. It
started to play *Für Elise*.

'This is Effie Cambray's music box,' Della said to herself.
'This could change everything!' She went to the dresser,
poured herself a stiff whiskey and sat down on the side of the
bed.

CHAPTER 15

'So, what do you all wanna do?' Mack Cambray asked the posse of twelve angry men as they stood by the Spencer's front steps. 'Jake Spencer's gonna be all right, yet you're behavin' like a lynch mob an' askin' me to support your actions. What if it wasn't Holden Bauldry or his men who shot Jake?'

'There's reports of rustlin' goin' on,' Mack pointed out, determined to keep up his challenge. 'Lot of livestock out there an' none of it branded anymore. Few snips through the barbed wire an' they're yours for the takin'.'

'Happened to my neighbour; lost several horses in one night, like that,' said one of the posse.

'An' what did yer neighbour do about it?' Mack asked.

'Blamed Holden Bauldry for it,' came back the reply. 'Cut his fences and stole some of his cattle in exchange. Tit for tat justice, mister. Made my neighbour feel good. He still goes on about it.'

'I know that Bauldry isn't the most pleasant man you're likely to come across, but why did your neighbour think that Bauldry was so short of horses that he needed to steal some of his?' Mack demanded to know.

''Cos Bauldry's a crook. What he's doin' ain't right.

Fencin' in all that land illegally. That's our children's grass he's takin'.'

'OK, I accept that,' Mack acknowledged firmly but calmly.

'The law ain't doin' nothin' about it,' someone else shouted out. 'Seems to me the law around here is developed afterwards.'

'That's a good observation,' Mack agreed. 'At first the government wanted cattlemen, but the industry grew too quickly for it, and now it wants settlers.'

'It's put us on a collision course, mister. This is becomin' not only a war between homesteaders and cattlemen but a war of rich cattlemen against poor ones.'

'Shouldn't be allowed, leasing of land to cattlemen. Favours the rich against the poor. If cattlemen want land they should have to get it in the same way that we've had to, through the Homestead Act. Claim your one hundred and sixty acres and show that you've improved it to get title.'

'Maybe, but it would kill off the cattle industry,' Mack pointed out. 'Cattle need a lot of grazing land. There'd be no beef, or what little there would be would be too expensive to buy.'

'So what?' someone else pointed out.

'Well, if I was a cattleman an' that was my livin' you were about to do away with, I wouldn't give it up without a fight.' Mack retorted.

'Bauldry's fences are cutting off our access to roads, and public grazin' and waterin' holes. That is illegal.'

'That's true,' Mack agreed. 'Look, you called me here to endorse your proposed actions to deal with these grievances. So back to my first question: what do yer wanna do about it?'

'Show Bauldry that he can't walk all over us by taking physical action against him. We start systematically cuttin' his illegal fences.'

'Yeah, that's right. We can't wait for the law to sort it out.'

'So when he finds out that you are the guilty party,' Mack responded, 'an' I guess you'll wan' him to know that, 'cos otherwise your action will be pointless, what do you think nice Mr Bauldry's gonna do next? How many of you think he'll come seekin' agreement as to which would be the best order to take his fences down?' No one raised their hand.

'OK, mister,' someone said, taking on the bait. 'He'll retaliate. Probably cut our fences: tit for tat justice again.'

'Do yer think that's all he would do?' Mack asked, emphasising the note of surprise in his voice for effect. 'Don't you think he might raise the stakes a bit as well to show you he won't be intimidated? How much do yer think he might raise them by?' The core speakers in the posse had a quick discussion between themselves before their spokesman stepped forward.

'He'd probably damage our crops – trample on 'em or possibly burn 'em.'

'An' if he did that, would you arrange to talk to him at that point and try and agree some rules as to how you might be able to live together? After all, as one of you already pointed out, that is how much of the law's developed out here. Doin' it that way ain't all bad, yer know.'

'Naw, mister. He'd think we're soft if we did that. He'd intimidate us even more. No, we'd have to raise the stakes and take further retaliatory action.'

'Such as?'

The core speakers had another quick debate amongst themselves.

'We'd torch some of his property,' the spokesman answered.

'So,' Mack sighed, 'I guess this escalation of violence will carry on, with people gettin' killed on one side eventually, then more people gettin' killed on the other until the community says, "this killin's gotta stop. We must sit down and talk!"'

A man at the back of the group started waving his shotgun in the air. 'I get what you're sayin', mister,' he shouted out, 'but you're denyin' our right to get angry! You can't do that!'

'Listen, all of you!' Mack said, raising his voice. 'I am not denyin' your right to get angry. I can understand why you are. I am not even denyin' your right to act on your anger but I am denying your right to act on it in an angry way!'

'OK. I have a point to make about the escalation of violence,' a tall, bearded man, known locally as Shorty, said calmly. He had chosen not to speak until now but had been following the debate intently. 'Violence would cease if Holden Bauldry was assassinated. Taken out of it. That Mose Alder couldn't replace him: made of far less aggressive stuff. That's where we see you comin' in, Mr Cambray, sir.'

'I'm happy to lead the campaign to resolve this situation, but I can assure you I ain't gonna go an' kill Holden Bauldry without talkin' to him first. That would be murder an' I don't intend dyin' with a noose aroun' mer neck, not now nor any time soon. You see, a lot of what you have told me today I'm afraid is conjecture based on anger and emotion. Things like assuming Bauldry's guilt over Jake Spencer and that Bauldry must have stolen the neighbour's horses. Bauldry is in danger of becoming a hate figure for you on which to project your fears. There's even a hint of jealousy that Bauldry's status in life has given him privileges that you don't have and would like. But on the other hand, you have given me some good grounds to take action. For example, as we all know, Bauldry ain't no saint. He has clearly sailed close to the wind in terms of legality in the way he has acquired a lot of the range for his ranch, in particular, preventing access to roads and parts of the public domain.

These are solid, factual grievances. I have some other things I would like to talk to him about and, with your permission, will add those to my list. In return, if he is interested in pursuing those conversations then he will have to guarantee not to harm us or our property and we will do the same.' Mack stopped talking and surveyed the silent gathering in front of him. 'Are you with me?' he asked. 'Those who ain't, raise your hand an' I will step down.'

The spokesman looked around his colleagues, making brief eye contact with each one as he did so. 'We're all with you, Mr Cambray,' he replied.

CHAPTER 16

It had been nearly a year since Mack Cambray had last set foot in Ramestown, and it had changed significantly, becoming a shadow of its former self. The only places that still remained open were part of the small block of buildings at the east end of Commercial Street. Supported by the increase in settlement of the area, the Wells Fargo office and the hardware and dry goods stores had managed to remain open.

Although trains still ran regularly on the railroad at the bottom of Main Street, they no longer stopped at Ramestown. After all, there was little point. There was no longer any demand from further afield to alight at Ramestown because apart from the small local stores there was no reason to go there. The hotel, the saloons and the theatre had all long since shut their doors. Even the Ramestown Cattlemen's Association had ceased to exist. Although Holden Bauldry had returned, the association's founder, Judd Rames, had permanently left the area. It was every man for himself now.

Mack sat in the bar area of what used to be the Ramestown Hotel. He stared up through the hole in the ceiling, and the roof above that, at the blue sky. The debris from the structural collapse lay littered around the far end

108

of the bar. The dust created by this and the winds that blew through the broken windows and flapping doors had settled for now in the warm, still air. Mack turned around as the eerie silence was broken by the heavy footfall of leather boots on the wooden floorboards.

'Holden!' Mack stood up and shook the cattleman's hand. 'How are you?'

'I'm fine, thanks. You?'

'Good, thanks.'

'I need a drink,' Holden said. 'There's whiskey in the cellar still. When this place shut its doors, everyone just up and left. Guess they wanted to travel light. I'll go an' dig us out a bottle of whiskey.' He came back with two bottles and passed one to Mack. 'Ain't no clean glasses anywhere so I got us a bottle each. Sorry to hear about the loss of your wife, by the way.'

'Thanks,' Mack said. 'I had trouble gettin' hold of you. Thought you'd gone to ground. Your ranch house appears to be fenced off. Then I thought of tryin' the Wells Fargo office.'

'You did right. I have, for all intents and purposes, gone to ground,' Holden said. 'Most of my communication is screened through the Wells Fargo. My house ain't completely fenced off, but you have to know your way through the maze of wire. I've sent my family to Denver for the time bein.' Safer there.'

'You soun' like a man expectin' trouble,' Mack commented.

'You're right, I am expectin' it, an' I guess that's why you might be here to talk to me. Like most of us, I've made some mistakes in my time but none so bad as believin' the open range would go on forever. Cost me dear. The last winter as near as dammit wiped me out. Had to borrow heavily against my property. Judd had the right idea: move to Texas, buy land and set up a ranch. I didn't get that at the time but I do now. But I can no longer afford to do that, so I've had to acquire land as best as I can. I'm a cattleman through an' through. Always have been; always will be. What we produce is still very much in demand all over the country. Cattle rearin' takes up a lot of land. Certainly not as much as it used to under open range, but a darn sight more than a one hundred and sixty acre homestead claim. An' I knew that some people, like your Settlers' Association, would object to that, hence me goin' to ground. Am I right?'

' 'Fraid so,' said Mack. 'They've got themselves pretty worked up about it all but I've managed to calm them down for the time bein'.'

'Well, you can tell 'em from me that I'd be happy to see any of 'em in court. They probably think that some of my fencin' in of public land is illegal but the precedent of prior possession I think suggests otherwise.' Although Mack didn't agree privately, he noticed the change in Holden Bauldry's attitude from the Ramestown boom years. Faced with the same situation then, Holden Bauldry would not even have considered going to court, let alone suggesting it. His way of defending his rights would have been by forcing his critics to stare down the barrel of a gun.

'What about fencing off roads and rights of access, such as in the Jake Spencer case?' Mack asked.

'We may have been overzealous in certain areas initially, but I'm sure that as our operation takes shape an' establishes itself we can roll those situations back. By the way, what happened to Jake Spencer wasn't anythin' to do with us. Dunno who it was. Could be gangs of small ranchers, or rustlers, even, tryin' to incriminate each other. It certainly wasn't us. I ain't lookin' for trouble, Mack, but if people wan' to give it to me, they'll get it back in spades.'

'Sure, I understand, Holden,' Mack replied.

'Have I given you enough to keep your settlers off my back?' Holden asked. 'I got better things to do than have to take them on.'

'No, you have, if you reaffirm their rights of access,' Mack replied.

'OK. Is there anythin' else?'

'Yes, but it's a personal matter.' Holden raised his eyebrows and nodded, indicating Mack to go ahead. 'Concerns your nephew Mose Alder and my wife's musical box.'

Holden Bauldry smiled. 'Huh,' he grunted. 'Yeah, I heard about that. Needless to say, Mose never stole that music box cos he was with me that night. An' that,' he said pointing and waving his index finger at Mack, 'is the honest truth. Interestin', though: before Comyn was set free, Mose did get a message from him. Comyn was askin' him to bring a gun to the jail so he could escape. There was a time when my nephew would have been gullible enough to do that but he's a lot more wised up these days.'

'Thanks for that,' Mack said. 'I thought that was the case, but it wouldn't have been fair to Effie to pass it up. We done?'

'Almost,' Holden replied. 'I don't wan' you to discuss this with your settlers but I have an idea you might be able to help me with.'

'Sounds interestin'. Go on,' Mack urged.

'I may not need all the land that I've fenced in. I need it at the moment because I have limited water resources and need unfettered access to them. I couldn't afford to have settlers restrict my access with their homestead claims. It would be a return to the fence cutting wars of old, when cattlemen cut settlers' fences.'

'I get that,' said Mack. 'So how can I help?'

'With your knowledge of water. I have in my mind a map of my ranch land with known sources of water marked on it, and potential sources of water worth exploring. Can you do that, or would you have to cover every inch of my land with your divining sticks?'

'I might be able to help you with that,' Mack replied, 'an' without coverin' every inch of ground. Lookin' at known sources of water and the land that lies between them in terms of its relief, soil an' rock type, an' greenness of vegetation can provide clues as to where the aquifers might run underground an' where to point the dowsin' sticks. I am happy to give it a go; after all, if you help me then I'll help you.'

'Good,' said Holden. 'Let's meet here again in two to three weeks. Contact me through the Wells Fargo office.'

'I have to try and find Mack Cambray, Judd,' Della said earnestly. 'Do you think this evidence could secure a conviction against that low-down rat Dean Comyn?'

'I am no lawyer, but I think it could do,' Judd replied. 'Do you wan' me to have a word with my legal people? They'll advise you as to the best thing to do.'

'No, not for the moment, thanks,' Della replied. 'I think Mack should know first. I am sure Effie would have wanted it that way. He should decide how best to pursue it. If I only knew where to look for him. I could talk to him; explain what has happened. You don't think he'd think I've been withholding evidence on purpose, do you? I'd genuinely forgotten that I had the music box in my enthusiasm to draw a veil over my old life and start anew.'

'I don't believe Mack would think that for a moment,' Judd reassured her. 'If you were tryin' to help Comyn you would never have refused to be his alibi in court.' He paused for a moment to think. 'I know,' he declared suddenly. 'I know how you might be able to make contact with Mack Cambray.'

'Oh, how, Judd?' Della asked eagerly.

'In two to three weeks' time, it's the first anniversary of Effie Cambray's funeral. She is buried in the Ramestown cemetery. Leaving a note in a message of condolence on her tombstone advisin' Mack that you want to see him would be a nice touch. Alternatively, I believe the Wells Fargo office is still open. If it is you could leave a message for Mack there. Put my name as a contact: don't use your address in case someone else picks it up.'

'Brilliant! Thanks, Judd. I would like to visit Effie's grave and leave the note there. It's more personal.'

CHAPTER 17

'You seem nervous tonight, Shorty. Anythin' the matter?'

'No, Mr Comyn, not really.' Shorty stared anxiously across the campfire at his inquisitor as he realized that he had just given the most stupid answer he could have.

'Not really!' Dean Comyn repeated, raising his voice. 'Well, either there's somethin' the matter, Shorty boy, or there ain't! So, which is it?'

'I sensed that I may have been bein' followed.'

'You may have been bein' followed. So what? You ain't done nothin' wrong. You're on public land helpin' a group of strangers work out who has cut a rancher's fence.'

'No, Mr Comyn,' Shorty replied meekly.

'No, Mr Comyn, indeed,' Dean repeated. 'Yer know what I think's botherin' yer, Shorty?' Shorty shook his head. 'I think you may have some bad news that you're afraid to tell me about. That little meetin' you an' yer fellow activists on the Settlers and Homesteaders' Association had the other day with Cambray. Am I right?'

'Yes, Mr Comyn.'

'Yes, Mr Comyn,' Dean mimicked. 'So, pull up a log, Shorty. Sit yerself down an' warm yerself in front of the fire.

Tell yer Uncle Dean all about it.'

Dean listened patiently to how Shorty explained that he had persuaded a group of a dozen activists to take action against Holden Bauldry's illegal enclosure of his proposed claim and the shooting of Jake Spencer, only for Mack Cambray to dissolve their resolve in a matter of minutes in favour of having talks with Bauldry. Dean Comyn shook his head in disgust.

From his vantage point on the hillside, Mack Cambray could survey the surrounding countryside. It was approaching dusk and the evening sunlight cast a maturity over the scenery before him that, under the circumstances, it didn't deserve. To the west he could see lights starting to appear in the homesteads. In front of him and extending to the east, he could see acres of pasture: pasture that used to be public domain but had since been enclosed by Holden Bauldry. Down below, Mack could see Bauldry's wire stretch away into the distance. He thought he might be able to see from this position if Bauldry had started work on his promised reparations but it was difficult to tell in the fading light.

As his eyes followed the wire's journey across the prairie, he thought he could see the occasional flicker of a flame from where the wire disappeared into a copse. He dismounted from his horse and, taking a small telescope out of his saddlebag, raised the glass to his eye. He saw what looked like a campfire with figures moving about around it. He refocused the scope but it was difficult to make out any more detail. As he lowered the instrument from his eye, he heard a double click in his left ear: that disconcerting double click as the hammer is pulled back twice and the chamber turns to line up the next bullet in the hammer's path. Mack instinctively turned his head towards the sound and felt the cold steel barrel of a gun against the lobe of his ear.

As Mack and his captor entered the small clearing in the copse and dismounted by the campfire, he found himself staring down the barrels of several guns. The scene was one of foreboding. The men around the campfire wore hoods so that they wouldn't be recognized. One hooded man was astride a stationary horse, standing up in the stirrups, his head in a noose. With his hands raised above his head, he kept his balance by holding onto the rope that was suspended from the branch above him and draped around his neck. Once the horse had been frightened off the man would effectively become responsible for his own death, the exact timing of which would be when his arms could no longer support his body weight. As his horse grunted a voice under the hood whimpered.

'Shut up, Shorty!' One of the hooded men snapped. Mack Cambray assumed Shorty was probably the settler who had challenged him earlier to kill Holden Bauldry.

'Who's that?' Mack asked. 'Why's he got a noose around his neck?'

'A rustler, a fence cutter,' the hooded man replied. We're a vigilante group tryin' to stamp that kind of behaviour out. These people will steal from anyone, settlers or big cattlemen. No law aroun' to stop it.'

'Cut 'im down,' Mack ordered. The man removed his hood. 'Dean, Dean Comyn,' Mack gasped.

'Yep, that's me, Mack Cambray. Dean Comyn.'

'Ain't seen you since . . . since before my wife died.'

'You reckon? I don't like other people messin' in my business. What were yer doin' out there snoopin' aroun'?'

'I saw your fire in the distance. Thought I'd take a look.'

'Did yer now? Like I say, I don't like people who sniff aroun' in other people's affairs.' Comyn took out his gun.

He placed the end of the barrel against Mack's forehead. 'I'm inclined to shoot such people.' He pulled back the hammer. 'So yer reckon you last saw me before your wife died?'

'Yeah,' said Mack.

'Well, you're wrong about that like you may be wrong about lots of other things. Which is why you shouldn't mess aroun' in other people's business.' Comyn released the hammer, removed the barrel from Cambray's forehead, span the gun around his index figure and re-holstered it. 'You see, the last time you saw me, Cambray, was several months back in Silver Mountain. You didn't recognize me. I had a beard then and my face was covered in blood. You were the man who chased off my attackers near the Globe Theatre.'

'I . . . I remember,' Mack Cambray stammered, shocked by Comyn's revelation.

'You saved my life that night, which is why I'm gonna spare you yours now. But then we're quits. Mess me with agen an' I'll kill yer. By the way, your wife, Effie . . . I didn't murder her that night. I didn't touch her either, but I had had a bit too much to drink, fortifyin' myself against the cold weather. She drew her gun on me; wanted me to leave. I was taken aback and, in my stupor, frightened that she might use it. I made a grab for it an' it went off accidentally in her hand. I never trusted that the court or the jury would even entertain the idea as a possibility, let alone believe such a simple truth. Their inbuilt prejudices were lookin' for a far more dramatic explanation. I may have been wrong not to trust their integrity. You may not even believe me. But that's the honest truth: take it or leave it. Now, get out of my life. Men, lower your guns an' let him ride out of here.'

*

Mack Cambray's head was spinning as he rode out of the copse. Should he believe Comyn? The man was clearly ruthless, totally self-centred, and no doubt capable of evil deeds but underneath, deep down perhaps, there was still some integrity, some sense of honour. If Comyn hadn't confessed to it, Mack would never have known that it was Comyn's life that he had saved that night. Mack's inclination was to believe that Effie's death was an accident. But, more importantly right now, there was another life at stake: that of the beleaguered Shorty.

Mack rode steadily through the copse, weaving his way through the trees to make it difficult for anyone to get a clear shot at him if Dean Comyn changed his mind. Once out of range, Mack stopped his horse under a tree and removed his Winchester rifle from its holster, hanging it over his shoulder. He then stood up on the back of his horse and hauled himself on to an overhanging branch. Balancing on the branch, he walked along it to the trunk, climbed a few feet up and then sat astride a thick branch on the other side of the tree with his back leaning up against the trunk. In the distance, he could see the glow of the campfire and the ill-fated Shorty, the noose still around his neck. Focusing specifically on the part of the rope above Shorty's hands, he aligned the sights, lowered and raised the lever and pulled the trigger.

'You spare someone their life an' that's how they thank you for it!' Dean Comyn shouted.

'Shall we go get 'im?' one of his men asked.

'No!' Comyn snapped. 'Cambray can wait. His time will come! Get after Shorty before he talks!'

It had all happened so quickly for Shorty: the crack of the gun, the tearing of the rope, his falling down into the saddle, the startled horse bolting, and Shorty grabbing its reins and digging his spurs into its body. But now he was clear of the copse and in control, with a few hundred yards start on his pursuers as he raced out across Holden Bauldry's ranch lands.

CHAPTER 18

Shorty followed Bauldry's barbed wire perimeter fence. He knew that eventually he must come across one of the repair teams. In this post-open range world, round ups and mending fences had become the stock in trade for cowboys. These small teams also acted as guards, but to a lesser degree, protecting the ranch's borders against fence cutters and rustlers.

Dusk was turning into night and, in spite of it being a full moon, gave Shorty some additional protection from his four pursuers, provided he kept to the shadows. He entered familiar territory. This was the land on which, only a few months ago, Shorty had proposed to claim one hundred and sixty acres worth for his wife and children. He was ready to go and make his claim, only to find that Holden Bauldry had already enclosed the land. The land office advised Shorty that he could still make the claim but he saw little point, as enforcement of his rights required the intervention of the courts and that was never going to happen anytime soon.

So he and his family had ended up where they were, on an inferior claim. Unfortunately, Shorty had a bitter streak, which laid dormant most of the time, but in his more vulnerable moments could be triggered by thoughts of victimhood. As a filter for absolving himself of any blame for his own actions and projecting his anger onto his enemies, it was very effective, but when it came to projecting his wrath on to Holden Bauldry, Shorty had allowed this delusory mental process to become an obsession of hate.

Hence, he had become an active voice in the Ramestown and District Settlers and Homesteaders' Association against the land grab by the large cattle ranchers. Some would have described him as a rabble-rouser but, regardless of the sophistication or otherwise of his oratory, Shorty was good at winning people round to his cause. Whereas previously he would have subscribed to his wife's view that, although Bauldy was grabbing land illegally, cutting his fences was also illegal and two wrongs did not make a right, the new Shorty argued his case differently. In a land where the rate of technological and social change outstripped the ability of lawmakers to develop appropriate laws and enforce them, then it became legitimate to fight fire with fire in order to survive. The attention he created did wonders for his self-confidence, and some of Shorty's neighbours thought that it had turned him into a completely new man, despite the underlying fragility of his rhetoric, which was based on little substance.

Blind to these issues, Shorty had become a man on a mission. It was he who found and convinced Dean Comyn that they should join forces, not the other way around. Everyone knew that Dean Comyn was trying to rebuild his life and present himself as a honourable and honest man, even if some were sceptical about his real intent. And Shorty saw him as a natural ally with shared interest: the settler and the small rancher who still needed access to the open range for their livestock against the big cattlemen. Naïve that Comyn might be just using him for more dubious means, Shorty had attracted people to their cause with a renewed passion. That was until Mack Cambray arrived on the scene and took Shorty's place as the people's orator, much to the chagrin of Shorty's new partner.

Unable to comprehend how his new friends of yesterday could suddenly turn into his sworn enemies of today, Shorty was running entirely on adrenaline. He had his wits about him sufficiently, however, to realize that he would need to stop soon and take a well-earned breather. He knew the geography of the land he had intended to claim pretty well, having spent much time surveying it and dreaming of how he might use it.

When he reached the junction with the narrow track, he decided to take it and leave the main trail. Although both routes ended up in much the same place, the track followed a far less circuitous path and the wooded slopes offered some protection from the moonlight that bathed the main trail in its luminescence. His pursuers, who would be travelling at speed and were unlikely to know of the track, would miss it and carry on the main trail. That would give Shorty a number of advantages: he could either gain further ground on his hunters, move off in an entirely different direction or hide in the rocks and woodland. He chose to gain further ground, hoping he might be able to find help, but if this strategy looked like failing he could always adopt plan B and hide. He removed the hood and noose from his head and threw them deep into the undergrowth, at the side of the track.

'There's somebody out there, Will,' Al said in a hushed voice.

'Yer sure?' Al replied. 'What makes yer say that?'

'Thought I heard twigs breakin'. Somethin' movin' slow. Cautious. A horse would be my bet.' They stamped out their fire. It was a good place to camp and they often bedded down there when on night patrol. Although they were on higher ground compared with the majority of Bauldry's ranch land, the rocks and trees provided shelter from the cold winds that could blow across the prairie at night. From their vantage point they still had a good view of the barbed wire fence, particularly as it stretched northwards.

Not that that really mattered. Most of the fence cutting and rustling took place at night and it was down to luck if the guards happened to catch someone up to no good on their particular patch. There were far too many miles of fencing to keep a constant watch on all of it. The main reason for sleeping out on warmer nights was to avoid the time wasted in travelling to and from better accommodation. Work had already started on refurbishing the line riders' huts for the winter.

Not for the first time that evening, Shorty was taken completely by surprise. Enjoying the cool night breeze on his face, he experienced a warm feeling of security that he had given his pursuers the slip. He was starting to feel human again, when a figure flying through the air knocked him clean off his horse and pinned him down on the ground. It had been a clever move: quick, effective and silent with no gunfire to warn any others who may have been in the area pursuing a related interest.

'On yer feet, mister,' said Al, as Will scurried down the bank towards them. 'Gently now.'

'He's lost his gun,' Will said as he patted Shorty down.

'They took it from me when they tried to hang me,' Shorty explained frantically.

'Who tried to hang yer?' Al asked.

'Dean Comyn an' his boys,' Shorty replied. 'They're after me. Four of 'em!'

'What yer done to upset them?'

'Disturbed 'em while they were tryin' to cut your fences and rustle your cattle.' A simple lie seemed more authentic and credible to tell under the circumstances, than an honest but complex truth, which might end up sounding contrived and unconvincing.

'Mighty noble of yer. Why would you wanna help us, mister. . . ?' Will's voice tailed away as they heard the distant droning thunder of horses' hoofs.

'Sounds like they're on the main trail,' Al interjected. They listened closely. The sound got louder, faded away then became louder again.

'They've turned around,' Will said. 'The main trail is moonlit an' they probably can't see him on it. Uh-oh,' he continued as the sound of hoofs stopped. 'They've probably discovered the track an' comin' up here!'

'Get 'im an' his horse outta sight! This could be a set up!' Al exclaimed. They stuffed Shorty's neckerchief in his mouth, bound his hands and feet and hid him and themselves in amongst the rocks. They cocked their rifles ready for action.

'They'll have to ride single file along here,' Will said. 'I'll take the first and third riders, you take the second and fourth, OK?'

'OK,' whispered Al. The two cowboys stayed very quiet and very calm. This wasn't the first stakeout they'd ever been involved in and they knew the drill. Their position was as good as it could possibly be. They were hidden behind the rocks, sheltered from the shafts of moonlight that danced through the trees onto the track in front of them. They glanced at each other as they heard the sound of approaching horses. The sound of the hoofs suggested they were barely moving at walking pace. It was as if their riders were busy scouring the undergrowth from their vantage point in

124

the saddle. Then the sound of movement stopped completely. Al and Will looked at each other again. Had the riders dismounted and proceeded off the track on foot? Had their natural instinct warned them that they might not be alone? Al and Will raised their rifles to their shoulders ready to fire.

Then the horses started moving again. The lead horse came slowly into view, the moonlight flickering across its face but no higher. Will aimed above the horse's head and fired. The bullet sped through the night air. There was no rider, just a rapid succession of return gunfire from the surrounding undergrowth. The hunted had now become the hunters. They had sacrificed their lead horse, which had bolted, but had, no doubt, held onto the other three.

Al thought quickly. Four riders, rustlers not gunmen, therefore probably only packing one gun each. Were they spread out or bunched together? With his rifle barrel resting in a crevice in the rock, he fired several bullets in a horizontal arc, his head well down below the top of the boulder. He peered through the crevice, praying that none of the shooters facing them were either accurate enough or lucky enough to get a bullet through it. His courage paid off and his reward was to see a narrow but quick burst of return fire, suggesting that the rustlers were spread out in a line, no longer than thirty yards from end to end. He signalled to Will with his hands that they should fire at that line in a pincer movement.

Al fired along the imaginary line from right to left and Will fired along it in the opposite direction. There was no return fire. They both fired along the line again. Still no return fire. Will signalled to Al that they should spread out and approach the line from opposite flanks. They moved slowly through the undergrowth, careful to keep out of the moonlight. A twig cracked under Al's foot as he moved. He fell to the ground and rolled away as far as he could from the spot where he had signalled his presence. Both men waited.

One solitary bullet was fired in return, suggesting one man still alive or potentially wounded. As Al and Will got closer to where they perceived the imaginary line to be, the breeze had slightly changed its direction, enabling moonlight to shower down through the trees onto the four bodies sprawled out on the ground.

Al arrived on the scene first. He turned over one of the bodies and bent down to remove the facemask. A hammer clicked behind him as its owner cocked his gun.

'You're a dead man walkin', mister,' the gun owner warned him. Will drew his gun as he slid down the bank and opened fire, hitting Al's potential assassin between the eyes.

'Well done, partner,' Al said.

'You turn 'em over, I'll keep yer covered,' Will replied. 'Can't be too careful with rustlers. Scum of the earth.' Al cautiously started to remove each rustler's hood but there was no longer anything to fear. All four of them were dead now.

'Who we got?' Will asked. 'Anyone we know?'

'I only recognize two of 'em: Frankie Osprey and Wildman Pete.'

'Both sidekicks of Dean Comyn,' Will added. 'C'mon. We'd better get back to Shorty an' find out how he got mixed up with this lot.'

It was ten minutes later when Holden Bauldry and his nephew, Mose, arrived on the scene. 'We heard the shootin',' Holden said. 'Came as quick as we could, but looks like you got it under control.'

'Yep. Guess so,' Al replied.

'We were down in the copse,' Mose explained. 'Fence been cut. Looks like they got away with forty of fifty cattle. If it continues we're gonna have to go to the expense of brandin' the whole herd.'

'See yer got a prisoner, then,' Holden observed. 'Anyone we might know?'

'Calls himself Shorty. Claims that Comyn an' his boys were tryin' to hang 'im when Mack Cambray arrived on the scene,' Will explained. 'Reckons it was thanks to Cambray's sharp shootin' that the rope got shot through an' he got away. I think he's lying somewhere along the line. Can't make mer mind up if he's tellin' the truth about stumblin' across Comyn cuttin' our fence, or if he's genuinely workin' for 'im.'

'Let me try to talkin' to him,' Holden Bauldry offered. 'If he is who I think he is an' he's been collaborating with rustlers, then the sentence for such a crime aroun' these parts is death by hangin'.'

'So, Shorty. You are who I thought might you be. You're the noisy one in that settlers' association ain't yer? The one who don't like me.'

Shorty sat there, saying nothing. He'd already been saved from being executed today and now a few hours later, if he wasn't careful, he was going to need saving again because someone else was after his blood. Shorty weighed up in his mind what was the best thing to do, the thing most likely to prolong his life. He acknowledged that Holden Bauldry wasn't the type to regard his silence as proof of innocence.

'OK, I have spoken out against you,' Shorty admitted. 'But you stole my claim.'

'I didn't steal your claim, Shorty. You hadn't made a claim at the time I fenced in that land. Nobody had cos I checked. So now that you've started bein' honest, let's revisit the part of your story about you catchin' Dean Comyn cuttin' our fence, so he decides to hang yer.'

127

'It's true, Mr Bauldry. It's as I tell it, honest it is.'

'No, it ain't, Shorty! Stop your darned lies! Rustlers work while wearin' hoods. It's so that they can't be recognized. If you'd stumbled across 'em they would have frightened you off, not tried to hang yer. So, did Comyn try to hang yer?'

'Yeah, too darned right he did!'

'Well, there can only be one reason as to why he did that, an' that's cos you either double-crossed him or let him down big time. Did yer promise you'd get your association members to join his side against me, eh? Is that it? An' thanks to Mack Cambray, you failed! I know these things you know. Not much misses my attention.' Shorty attempted to mumble some reply, some last-ditch attempt to finding a mitigating circumstance for his behaviour, but the right words wouldn't fall out of his mouth. He looked a broken man.

Just before he turned to walk away, Holden Bauldry shot Shorty in the back of the head. Mose stared at him, speechless.

'I should have hung him for what he'd done,' Bauldry said, dismissing his nephew's stare. 'But somehow, that seemed less cruel.'

CHAPTER 19

'What's that on the other side of the railroad, Seth? Strung up over there?'

Seth steered the wagon slowly over the rough ground. He welcomed their fortnightly trip to the Ramestown dry goods and hardware store. It was a day out away from the toil of the homestead. Besides, he and Bart picked up a few essentials for the neighbours as well, an errand for which they got paid sufficient to buy a bottle of whiskey, enough to wet their whistle on the return journey.

'Dunno,' Seth said, employing one of his favourite words with a hint of resignation in his voice. Several years eking out a living on the frontier had taught him not to be surprised by anything. He took his small but treasured telescope from his pocket and passed it to Bart.

'Holy smoke,' said Bart, readjusting the focus to make sure his eyes weren't deceiving him. 'Looks like there's been a hangin' party. We'd better take a closer look!'

Seth and Bart stared at the bodies of the five men who curiously looked like they'd been shot and then suspended from a gantry at the end of the railroad platform in some macabre form of public spectacle. They climbed down from their wagon to take a closer look and walked around the back of

129

the bodies. Each body had a placard on its back with the word 'RUSTLER' painted on it in a blood red colour.

'That one on the end has been shot in the back of the head,' Bart pointed out. Seth walked around the front of the corpse and stared up the face's gnarled features, which suggested that he had died a frightened man.

'That's Shorty, that is,' Seth pointed out in an indignant tone. 'Whoever did this couldn't even be bothered to close his eyes afterwards.'

'He wasn't no rustler,' Bart said authoritatively.

'Dunno,' said Seth. 'He seemed to have it in for Holden Bauldry and, accordin' to popular rumour, had links with the Comyn gang.'

'Dah, he was all talk, no action, Shorty was,' Bart said in judgement. 'Didn't deserve a death like this though, jest fer sayin' things. Guess we'd better take his body back in the wagon.'

'Dunno if there'll be room,' Seth said. 'Might have to make a separate trip. I don't mean this in a bad way but I think his ol' lady would be more grateful to have her provisions than a dead body an' no provisions.'

'Whatever way, this is gonna unsettle the homesteaders. They ain't used to this sort of thing. This don't bode well,' Bart pointed out.

Dean Comyn rode into Ramestown as fast as he could. Although he lived a nomadic existence on the open range he kept close counsel with his network of cronies who acted as his eyes and ears. Five men, including Shorty, had left his campfire the other night and none of them had returned. But deep inside, he knew that this journey was not one of speculation as to what had happened to these five men, but one of confirmation.

Dean stared up at the five bodies hanging from the

gantry, anger in his eyes. This was the work of Holden Bauldry and an act of war. If his men had just been shot while doing their work, then Dean could have lived with that. After all, getting caught was just an occupational hazard of being a rustler. But this! This was different. This was a public humiliation. Dean took out his Colt and, fanning the hammer slowly, let off four bullets. One after another, his four men fell to the ground as the bullets shattered each of the ropes with which they had been suspended from the gantry. The shopkeeper from the hardware store came running down Main Street carrying his rifle.

'Oh, it's you, Mr Comyn. Wondered what was goin' on.'

'Jest cuttin' my men down. D'yer know who did this?'

'No, I don't,' the storekeeper replied. 'Happened in the middle of the night. Didn't hear a thing.'

'How much yer charge to bury these boys' bodies on Boot Hill?'

'Pauper's burial?'

'Yeah. These men's achievements in life were insufficient to warrant a coffin.'

'Well, let me see. The ground's hard up there at this time of year. What about two dollars a body?'

'You drive a hard bargain, but OK.'

'What about the fifth man? Don' yer wan' me to bury him?'

'Nope! He's the only one who deserves to be strung up there on public display. Tell yer what. For an extra dollar, you can take that placard off his back. He weren't no rustler. I wan' yer to make up a new placard for him. Paint on it the word "TRAITOR", cos that's what he was, an' leave 'im hangin' there for all the world to see!'

Holden Bauldry took the message personally from the Wells Fargo rider. Mack wanted to see him a week today in the hotel in Ramestown to discuss the latest developments, including searching for more water. He wrote an equally brief acceptance and gave it to the rider to take back. If he had been expecting some reaction from Mack to the men he'd hung from the gantry at the Ramestown railroad station then Holden was disappointed by Mack's note. It would have been unfair to describe the invitation to meet as terse but it was certainly short and gave nothing away. Typical of Mack Cambray to keep his powder dry, Holden thought. He must have heard about the public exhibition of dead rustlers and known it was Holden behind it. Was he angry? And mentioning 'searching for more water' . . . Was that off the table now or still on it?

Holden had made his point violently but clearly to the local community: don't mess with Holden Bauldry. As far as he was concerned, that was the end of the matter. If other people wanted to rake over the ashes then it was their problem if they got burnt. Besides, if there was nothing that he could do about it, Holden certainly wasn't the type of man to worry about it. His final thought on the matter was that Mose should come to the meet with him. The young man was inoffensive enough, albeit this was part of his problem growing up. However, Mose's mild nature could have a calming effect if Mack was angry. Besides, it would do the boy no harm to see and learn how grown men negotiate. After that Holden paid the situation no more mind.

Mack Cambray was starting to feel more optimistic about the planned meeting with Holden Bauldry. He'd worked his way through the difficult bit with the local settlers; everyone had accepted that Bauldry had instigated the deaths of Shorty and the four other men. Initially there was anger and a call to arms, but the sheer violence surrounding the untimely deaths of these men had an unsettling effect on these people who were basically peace-loving farmers. They began to realize that if they were to take on Holden Bauldry in a physical fight then they would have to punch way above their weight if they didn't want to end up as losers.

Mack explained to them that if they felt the need for a physical fight, the person to take it to was Dean Comyn. He described to them in some detail how he had discovered Shorty with a noose around his neck in Comyn's camp and how he'd managed to set him free. The thought of taking on the heartless Comyn with his evil reputation unsettled them even more and it was then that the settlers accepted Mack's reassurance that he and Holden Bauldry would resolve the 'Comyn problem' between them.

That left the other problem of convincing Holden Bauldry to release some of his land to the settlers as, in effect, a peace offering. It was in that area, however, that Mack started to feel optimistic. He had managed to obtain a topographical map of the area from one of the land claims surveyors and had diligently marked on it all known sources of water discharge and whether they were natural, such as springs or streams, or man-made, such as wells. Of the latter, he had particularly good knowledge, given that he had recommended many suitable sites and subsequently supervised much of the digging. Mack then started marking the map with the sites of those trees and shrubs that he had observed had remained green during periods of drought, suggesting ground water nearby. Finally, he was able to begin work on the most time-consuming activity: identifying the various soil and rock types and colouring them on the chart using different colours depending on their porosity. It was this final piece of work, albeit in combination with the others, that started to unlock the secrets of where water might be flowing underground in hidden aquifers between the low-lying discharge points and the higher level, porous recharge points.

It certainly wasn't an accurate science, but with the aid of site visits and the use of his divining rods, Mack was confident that he would be able to determine potential well sites for test drilling on Holden Bauldry's land.

Dean Comyn was becoming impatient. Unable to find out who was responsible for the stringing up of his men from the owner of the hardware store, he had tried the Wells Fargo office. A dollar bill bought some success.

'It was Bauldry that strung 'em up,' the clerk advised, grateful for the bonus. 'I didn't see it but my colleague did. He tol' me about it. Middle of the night. The men were already dead. Anyway, like I say, Bauldry an' some of his men, strung 'em up an' then put the placards on 'em.' The clerk started to repeat himself hoping somewhat naively, that the more he spoke, the more likely Dean Comyn was to think that he was getting value for money. This outlaw Comyn was clearly not one to end up on the wrong side of.

Comyn pushed forward the palm of his hand, signalling to the clerk that it was time to shut up. 'An' how will I find Mr Bauldry?' he asked with a sneer on his face. The clerk hesitated. Bauldry had told all those working at the Wells Fargo office that on no account were they to disclose his address to anyone. Dean Comyn peeled off another dollar bill and passed it to the clerk, who realized that if ever there was a time to think on his feet, it was now.

'He comes to town now an' agen,' the clerk replied, 'Could be comin' soon,' he added quickly.

'Oh?' Dean said, sounding curious and surprised. The clerk cleared his throat to speak, knowing that he hadn't given sufficient information as yet to retain his second dollar bill.

'He meets occasionally here with Mack Cambray. Cambray's invited him to another meet at 10am Wednesday week in the hotel. Well, what's left of it.'

'Has he accepted it?' Dean Comyn asked with a smile on his face.

'Dunno, the rider should be back soon with his reply.'

'When? Before sundown?'

'Oh yes,' said the clerk positively. 'Can't say precisely. Getting' messages to and from Bauldry ain't easy. Complicated set of dead letterbox drops,' he lied. 'You understan'?'

Dean Comyn nodded his head in agreement. Whether he understood or not was irrelevant. He'd much rather meet Holden Bauldry on the neutral ground of Ramestown than on Bauldry's home turf. Mack Cambray, as well. That just left Della Peveril and then Dean would be even with the world.

'Let me know when your rider gets in,' he said to the clerk. 'I'll be over in the hotel, remindin' meself of what the old place looks like.'

Della Peveril felt more at ease than she had felt for days. Her arrangements were now all in place and her tickets booked. Her school would remain open for the few days she was away, thanks to the good offices of a group of parents. At last, she could gain closure on the death of Effie Cambray and many of the problems that that unfortunate episode had brought into her life.

Judd had offered to send one of his men with her as a chaperone but she had fewer fears about her safety than Judd did. After all, she would be in company virtually all the journey, on the overnight train north and then the early morning stagecoach that stopped at Ramestown on its journey east. That gave her half an hour to visit the grave and make her way back to the Wells Fargo office to catch the service west. Perfect, Della thought to herself. She was looking forward to her visit Wednesday week.

CHAPTER 20

'Well, all that remains, boys, is to await the arrival of our guests,' Dean Comyn said to his three sidekicks. 'Everythin' else is now in place ready for the party to begin. Things are lookin' good. Help yerself to some whiskey before show time,' Dean added with magnanimity. 'Bring up a few bottles from the bar,' he ordered Trigger.

'Where did yer have the boys buried?' Mex asked.

'Up on Boot Hill at the back. Why?' Dean enquired.

'Me an' Hobo would like to pay our respects once we've had a drink. Couple of 'em was personal friends of ours. Is it far?'

'Few minutes walk, behind the Wells Fargo office. Very 'onourable of you,' Dean commented.

Ramestown had had a far shorter life than many of its residents and their neighbours in the surrounding environs. As a consequence, Boot Hill was not a crowded cemetery and Della found it easy to find Effie Cambray's tombstone. She had picked some wild flowers that were growing by the side of the road when she alighted from the stagecoach, and arranged them ceremoniously on Effie's grave. Della placed her note to Mack in a small oilskin bag and laid it on top of the grave under a small rock. She then knelt down at the

136

foot of the grave, closed her eyes and prayed silently for Effie's soul.

'The boss maybe a bit of a bastard at times but at least he didn't skimp on the boys' graves,' said Mex philosophically as he and Hobo sat on the end of one of their dead colleague's graves.

'How'd yer mean?' Hobo asked.

'Well he's given each of the boy's a separate grave. Could have thrown their bodies in one big pit. Shows respect that does.'

'S'pose so,' Hobo commented.

'Well, it shows more respect than you're showing that woman attendin' that grave up there,' Mex continued. 'You shouldn't be lookin' at her like that,' he teased. 'Looks of that sort are alright in the dance hall but not here.'

'I ain't lookin' at her like nothin',' Hobo replied. 'She looks familiar; I think I know her.'

'You think you know her?' Mex questioned. 'You could never get to know a woman like that,' he continued as he, too, stared at the slim, hourglass figure dressed in elegant, fashionable clothing.

'She used to work here. A song and dance girl in the local bars. Ah, what's her name?'

'It's Peveril!' Mex exclaimed. 'Della Peveril. She used to be the boss' woman.'

'An' he's always said he'd have a strong word with her if he ever saw her again,' Hobo added.

As Della opened her eyes and stood up, she sensed she was being watched. She turned her head round slowly in both directions but there was no one there: apart from herself the graveyard was empty. She turned back to take one last look at Effie's grave. As she did so, she stroked her left thigh subtly to check that her pocket Derringer was still secure. The feel of its solid shape under her dress gave her confidence and, as she slowly exhaled, she turned to go.

'Not so fast, lady!' She felt two hot sweaty hands, one on each shoulder. She moved her left hand down to her thigh but it was quickly restrained and hoisted up behind her back.

'What you hidin' under your skirts there?' Hobo asked, struggling to pat Della down while he restrained her.

'I wouldn't go touchin' 'er like that! Mex interjected sharply. 'The boss wouldn't be too pleased if you'd been treatin' his woman the way you treat some of yer own.'

'I ain't touchin' her like anythin',' Hobo said defensively. 'Thought he she might be packin' a gun, that's all.'

'Packin' a gun? A pretty thing like her? She wouldn't know how to use one,' Mex sniggered.

'Who are you? What do you want?' Della demanded in her most authoritative school ma'am voice. 'What boss?'

'The boss, ma'am,' Mex replied. 'Your number one fan: Dean Comyn!'

The two men frogmarched Della down to the hotel where Mex disappeared and a rough, unwashed man by the name of Trigger helped Hobo bundle her upstairs to a room on the top floor where she was pushed onto a flea-bitten mattress on the bed.

' 'Fraid there's no workin' lock on the door, ma'am,' Hobo pointed out. 'Leastways, we can't find the key. We're expectin' some bad customers comin' to town, you see. So, for your own safety, I suggest you stay in this room. I wouldn't try an' come out if I were you, cos we're removin' the floorboards from outside yer door. We'll put 'em back when we wanna come see you. Otherwise, if yer come out in a hurry, you'll go crashing through the ceiling of the floor below. Unlikely to kill yerself, mind, but you'll probably break a few bones an' there ain't no doc out here anymore. Left town like everybody else. Anyway, that aside, make yerself at home. I'm sure the boss will be up to see you shortly.'

Della stared around the room. She recognized it as her old one when she lived at the hotel. But it had changed significantly. The only piece of furniture apart from the bed and mattress was the set of dressing room drawers, except now some of the handles were missing and many of the drawer bases were broken, rendering them useless. Like the rest of the room, everywhere was covered in dust thanks to the broken windows and the missing section of ceiling and roof in one corner of the room. Birds seemed to fly in and out at their leisure, which explained why the faded blue curtains that flapped around in the breeze were covered in bird droppings. The wallpaper by the windows was hanging off the walls, which were all stained and covered with patches of mould. Della was still in a state of shock when there was a knock on the door.

'Well, well, well!' said Dean Comyn. 'If it ain't Della Peveril. Couldn't keep away, huh? Your presence would have been very welcome aroun' here about a year ago, but better late than never.'

'I'm sorry, Dean, but I couldn't have gone through with the alibi. I could never have lived with myself. Anyway, you got off, didn't you?' she challenged, desperately trying to get Dean to reframe his perspective on what had happened. 'My absence from the court wasn't the big deal it was probably made out to be at the time. The truth always comes out eventually.'

'And so it might,' Dean retorted. 'But you put me through hell. As did Holden Bauldry, and he continues to do so. You find out who your friends are when the chips are down. Yet here you are. Fate has decreed that today you have chosen to walk back into my life, as has Holden Bauldry and as has Mack Cambray. The three people who have attempted to destroy me.' He placed his hand under Della's chin and squeezed hard. 'You see, Della: you, Bauldry and Cambray don't know what it's like to go through a trial, be found guilty and virtually have the noose placed around your neck before you are set free. You don't understand the fear of that or the indignity. Yet!' he said, pushing her away.

'What do you mean, "yet"?' Della spluttered. 'What . . . what are you going to do?'

'Today, I have arranged for three showcase trials to be held in this hotel, one after the other, to teach those involved how equitable justice can be achieved without having to game the system. First there will be the case of Holden Bauldry: a career bully and intimidator, and a stealer of the people's commons. Maximum penalty, if found guilty: death by hangin'! Then there is the trial of Mack Cambray. A meddler who takes the law into his own hands, believing that his idea of justice is the only notion permissible and, consequently, is the cause of much unnecessary collateral damage. Maximum penalty, if found guilty: a bullet through the heart. Which brings me to you, sweet Della, the third defendant in my showcase trials.'

'What am I accused of? You are not going to kill me as well, are you?' Della exclaimed. Dean held his hand up, signalling for her to be quiet.

'You are accused of being judgemental in the first degree, to an extent where you do not even try to find out all the facts first and make assumptions of a circumstantial nature. In this instance that could have caused an innocent man – me – to lose my life, if it hadn't of been for a simple twist of fate. Maximum penalty if found guilty. . . .' He paused to watch and enjoy the look of horror on her face, 'Don't be afraid. It is not death. I am nothing if I am not merciful. It will be a sentence to a lifetime of subservience to those you have wronged. You may, while you sit here over the next few hours contemplating your defence, consider appropriate ways as to how you might fulfil your sentence and ease the suffering of those you have harmed through your impulsive nature!'

'Merciful!' Della hissed in disbelief. 'So how do you plan to show that side of your nature to Holden Bauldry and Mack Cambray if you intend to kill them?'

'Their deaths will be mercy killings. They are too far gone, too arrogant to show contrition. I don't believe you are, however. That's the difference!' He shut the door quietly and was gone.

Holden Bauldry rode slowly into Ramestown that Wednesday morning. He was a man deep in thought. His planned meeting that day was going to be critical, not just for his own future, but for many other people besides. If it went well there could be peace in the district. A loose peace, perhaps, but one where everybody could rub along with each other, more or less. More or less was probably as good as it was ever going to get, but that, given the alternative, would be good enough. Otherwise, it was going to be a three-sided war between the big ranchers like himself, the settlers and the small ranchers, and the likes of Dean Comyn – the rustlers.

Holden knew that Comyn held the key to the future prosperity of the Ramestown district. As more people came west, encouraged by the federal government through the Homestead Act and similar legislation, land was becoming scarcer and scarcer, so everyone was seeking title to their own patch. The public commons – the open range – was shrinking rapidly as more and more of it came under private ownership.

At first it was just the early settlers that created this problem, but this sector of the population was continually increasing as more and more immigrants came west. Also, there were the big cattlemen, those with large herds that used to be open rangers until, following big losses in the severe winters of '85 to '86 and '87, they eventually realized that their model of operation was not the most efficient, and fencing in land for their exclusive use was actually more effective. That left those who still relied on open range, the homesteaders that wanted somewhere for their livestock to graze, the sheep men, the small ranchers: cattlemen that could not afford to buy their own land, and the rustlers such as Comyn. The latter were a headache for everyone, and Bauldry's minimum negotiating objective from the day was to agree a coalition of all other parties involved to have rustlers forcibly removed from the range. Then the coalition members should find it easier to rub along.

Lost in his own thoughts, Holden had failed to realize that he had traded some awareness of what was going on around him. He had almost forgotten that his nephew Mose Alder was following dutifully a few yards behind him. He had missed the fact that the window blind in the Wells Fargo office, which was always kept open, had been fully pulled down. Mose hadn't. Although he hadn't set foot in Ramestown since its demise, it seemed odd to him to have the blind down when the window was in the shade but the office was supposedly open. Mose also observed that the hardware and dry goods stores looked closed and had boarded up their windows. It was as if the people that ran all three premises were expecting some sort of trouble. He imagined the three monkeys: 'speak no evil, hear no evil, see no evil'.

Similarly, Holden hadn't noticed the four horses grazing in the corral at the back of the jail. Mose had. He noticed that they weren't saddled, indicating that their owner or owners were on more than just a flying visit to town.

'Right, boy,' Holden said to Mose as they dismounted outside the Ramestown Hotel. 'Leave the talkin' to me. You just sit and listen and learn. This is about negotiatin'. Givin' somethin' up to the other guy that you can afford to lose in return for somethin' you want more.' They strode side-by-side through the bat wing doors, neither of them expecting to hear the sound of revolvers being cocked from behind each door.

'Mornin,' boys!' Dean Comyn appeared from behind the counter of the bar. 'Drop yer guns!' Holden Bauldry and his nephew did as they were told.

'What you doin' here, Comyn?' said Bauldry, spitting the words out of his mouth as if each one had a nasty taste.

'Heard you were comin', Bauldry. Wanted to talk to yer about the murder of some of my men. Yer see, I think you're guilty, but I need to be sure before I hang yer. Ask you a few questions about it.'

'That's a matter for the law!' Bauldry replied angrily.

'Huh, the law . . . Where's the law when yer need it, eh? The law aroun' here gets developed too damned slow, an' often after the fact. You an' I both know that, Bauldry. The people make the law, not the lawyers. Devoid of imagination, they jest codify the things we do best and that promotes, in their opinion, how people should get along with each other. As they will no doubt do regardin' the recent murder of my men, after you an' I decide what is right and what is wrong. Trigger, lock the young lad in the jail an' stay down there with 'im an' the horses. After all is said and done, you ain't gonna help yer case by callin' on your nephew, a biased witness, are you, Bauldry? If I've any understandin' of the law from personal experience, I don't believe that that's the way it's supposed to work.'

Mose Alder felt very dispirited as he sat in the cell of the small Ramestown jailhouse. His uncle's hard talk and bluster had failed to free him so far. Here he was stuck on his own, and for how long he had no idea. Just him and his mind. There were no other distractions. Apart from the horses occasionally whinnying in the corral, there was no sign of life outside his cell window. The view inside the jail was less dynamic than the one outside. The gun cage was completely empty, which presumably occurred a long while ago, and the shelves devoid of any files or paperwork. Four saddles and saddle-bags had been dumped on the floor, which Mose guessed belonged to Comyn and his three stooges.

He didn't even have any one to talk to. Trigger had fallen asleep in the sheriff's chair. It was still only half past nine in the morning, but his jailer had managed to work his way through half a bottle of whiskey already. So Mose started thinking. The meeting was due to start at ten, which meant that Mack Cambray should hopefully arrive soon, and if Mose remembered correctly where the Cambray homestead was situated, Mack should be arriving from a westerly direction. Mose wondered how he might be able to attract Mack's attention without waking the 'sleeping beauty' next door.

Mack Cambray rode at a canter as he approached Ramestown, the brim of his hat pulled down low over his eyes to protect them from the morning sun. Regardless, he scanned the horizon and the buildings continually for any signs of anything untoward. It was a natural habit he had acquired as a line rider, constantly looking for stray cattle, wolves, rustlers or any other potential threat to his well being when he was alone in the wilderness. That was how he became alerted to a flashing light coming from the south of

144

the town. It was clearly someone signalling, using some shiny object to reflect the sunlight. Three short bursts, then nothing. The pattern kept repeating. Mack knew that if someone was trying to imitate the use of smoke signals, they were signalling that something was wrong.

As Mack rode slowly across to the jail, Mose threaded his belt back through the loops on the waistband of his pants. His brass belt buckle had done the trick. Standing at the window, Mose raised his index finger to his lips to indicate that there was someone else present. The two men proceeded to speak in a whisper.

Having agreed on some sort of plan, Mack left his revolver on the sill of the cell window for Mose to take. He decided to leave his own horse in the corral and proceed on foot with just his rifle. Mack wondered if he had done the right thing in giving his gun to Mose. His revolver could fire more bullets than his rifle could in the same amount of time. On the other hand, if Mose could take care of his jailer then it evened up the odds against the Comyn gang. On hearing Mose's tale of events, Mack decided not to walk into the saloon but to approach the hotel from the other side, where his entrance might have more of an element of surprise. As he turned the corner into Commercial Street, the silence was almost deathly. There was no birdsong, just the sound of a slight breeze blowing round the desolate buildings and along the alleyways. Every time he stepped forward on the gritty, dusty street, the sound of his footfall reminded him of the distant rumble of thunder.

'Drop it, Cambray!' a voice above him shouted out. Having already cocked the Winchester after he had dismounted, Mack swung it round and up as quickly as possible. At the end of the rifle's sights, he saw the smirking figure of Dean Comyn staring out of an upstairs window, his left forearm around Della Peveril's throat and his right hand holding a gun to her head. Mack laid down his rifle.

Mose checked Trigger was still sleeping and, picking up the pillow off his cell bed, held it flat against his stomach. He then took the firearm from the windowsill and placed it between his body and the pillow. Mose had never even attempted to kill a man before let alone actually shot one. He took a deep breath to steel himself: he knew that if he didn't step up now, he probably never would, and the gossip and rumours that people sometimes spread about him would become regarded as the truth. His rite of passage to manhood had arrived and he knew that couldn't afford to fluff his lines.

'Wake up, scumbag!' Mose shouted. Trigger stirred. 'I wanna drink,' Mose continued. 'Too damned hot and stuffy in here!'

'All right, all right! Keep yer hair on, young'un,' Trigger said. He got up from the table and went over to one of the saddlebags and took out a water bottle. 'Here,' he said walking back to the cell. Trigger held the bottle through the bars for Mose to take. There was a muffled explosion as Mose fired the gun through the pillow. Thanks to the gun pointing slightly upwards, the bullet hit Trigger in the chest. He fell to the ground dead. Mose fired a second bullet through the pillow at the cell lock. As the smoke started to fade, he kicked the cell door open. Standing over the dead man, he picked up the rifle of his first kill and then removed Trigger's gun belt before strapping it on himself. Stuffing Mack's revolver into his waistband, Mose took one last look out of the cell window. Apart from the horses in the corral and the breeze, nothing moved outside. He was free at last. Outside, he removed the lasso from one of the horses, put it across his shoulder and made for the hotel.

'If you're thinking of trying to escape with the girl, Cambray, you'll need a good sense of balance, cos some of the joists are rotten!' Dean Comyn pointed out as Hobo removed the floorboards to prevent their prisoners from escaping. 'Besides, we're only gonna be next door, conductin' the trial of Holden Bauldry for his crimes against the common people!'

The removal of the floorboards from outside their prison room held some advantages for Della and Mack. It meant that one of them could stand watch at the open door, with a good view down the long corridor, to see if their captors were approaching with intent, to replace the floorboards and enter the room.

Those extra few seconds warning, compared with the time taken to unlock the door, proved their value immediately. While Della had stood guard, Mack had systematically surveyed the whole room looking for any resources that might help them in an escape bid, but had only managed to find some sheets of writing paper and a pencil in the chest of drawers. Disheartened, he wandered over to the window just as Mose came around the corner below.

'It's Mose!' he whispered to Della as quietly as he could. 'He must have broken out of jail!'

'No one coming,' she whispered in return. Mack acted quickly. He needed to attract Mose's attention. He grabbed hold of one of the faded blue curtains and pushed it through the hole in the broken window where it immediately started flapping around in the breeze and caught Mose's eye. He looked up and saw Mack Cambray's head leaning out of the window, with his right index finger against his lips to signify that they couldn't afford to make a noise.

147

He then signalled to Mose to wait there while he disappeared briefly before returning to the window with a sheet of the writing paper and the pencil. Mack indicated to Mose that he was going to write him a message. Hastily, he scribbled down the following:

> *Holden about to undergo a mock trial. Della with me – we are prisoners in this room. Best escape is through the window but need rope. When curtain hanging outside window, safe to communicate. Good if you can lay your hands on some guns. Store them in the livery stable up the road.*

Mack screwed the note into a ball and threw it down to Mose. He caught it before it hit the ground and unravelled the piece of paper. *Brilliant*, Mack thought. *We have a communication system in place.* Mose offered Mack the rope across his shoulder silently, to which Mack gave him the thumbs up.

'All clear?' Mack whispered to Della. She nodded quietly. When Mack indicated that the coast was clear, Mose removed the rope from his shoulder, knotted one end and then swung it backwards and forwards like a pendulum. As the rope gained its own momentum, he threw it high into the air. Avoiding the shards of glass in the broken windowpane with his outstretched arm, Mack caught the rope on the second attempt and pulled it in through the window. He coiled the rope and, carefully passing it back through the broken glass again, he placed it on the flat roof above the window next to Della's pocket gun, safe from prying eyes.

CHAPTER 21

'So, Holden Bauldry, you stand accused of violating people's property, personal safety and stealin' land that belongs to everybody for your own personal gain. How do you plead?' Dean Comyn felt in his element, about to correct the injustices of world, as he perceived them.

'You're a mad bastard, Comyn,' Bauldry retorted. 'You're not above the law. You ain't got no authority to run a trial in any damned court, let alone this one!'

'Seems to me that you're lookin' at this all wrong, Bauldry. I ain't the one tied to a chair, unable to move. I ain't the one without a gun.' Dean removed his revolver from its holster and pulling back the hammer, held the end of the barrel against Bauldry's temple. 'Seems to me that I got all the authority aroun' here I need, an' you got none. What d'yer say, boys?' Mex and Hobo nodded and mumbled their affirmations, not sure whether this was going to be an entertaining mockery of the accused, in which case they could relax, or the boss strutting his ego and trying to be clever, which would mean they would have to keep their wits about them.

'I sure ain't pleadin' guilty to any so-called crime you're gonna accuse me of, Comyn,' Bauldry answered.

'That's your choice,' Dean Comyn said dismissively, 'but

tell me, weren't you responsible for the Blake family leavin' the area? Didn't you organise the cuttin' of their fences so that your cattle could take a short cut across their land, crushing their crops in the process in order to access a waterin' hole?

'While you think about your defence to that charge, let me ask you about another instance. Didn't you also plan for the removal of the Cambrays shortly after their arrival? I remember you tellin' me that the Cambrays should be easy to get rid of. Some washed up line rider, an outta work cowboy down on his luck, you said. Mack Cambray might know somethin' about mindin' cattle but sure as hell would know nothin' about how tough homesteadin' is. You got that one wrong, but then again your judgement's always been your achilles heel, ain't it?'

'You know I organised those two particular intimidations, Comyn, 'cos I asked you to carry 'em out!' Bauldry said angrily. 'What's yer point?'

'My point is that you knew what you did was wrong in the eyes of the law, which was why you never supported me when I was on trial. You didn't want the stuff that you were responsible for comin' out in court, 'cos it might damage your reputation!'

'The court wouldn't have understood. I had a livelihood to protect. Not just mine but my workers and their families. Us cattlemen were on the open range before the homesteaders. Our success helped justify building the early railroads to get our product to market, which everyone else, particularly in the east, was clamouring for. The federal government put us in a no-win situation. They wanted a successful cattle industry but they wanted farmers an' settlers on the same land. Eventually, the land was gonna run out an' start trouble. As it turns out, Texas had the right idea. Ration the land by allowin' people to buy title to it or lease it from someone else who could afford to buy title to it.' But elsewhere the federal government didn't do that. They put us on a collision course with all the settlers comin' west. They didn't seem to understand how much grazin' land an' access to water that cattle need. God knows we did cut back on that after the big die-up in those two really bad winters. We found by fencin' in that we didn't need as much land an' could be more efficient than when it was all open range. We changed – we did out bit!' Holden Bauldry pointed out in earnest.

'You did your bit when you started fencin' in the range and creatin' ranches,' Dean Comyn repeated, slowly and deliberately. 'You claimed homestead land in other people's names, who you funded, for your ranch. The legality of that is dubious; the morality of it is not. Some of the land you fenced in for your ranch you no doubt have a perfect legitimate claim to. For example, if you purchased or leased railroad land, but some of it where you just fenced in the public commons, you effectively stole land that wasn't yours to take.'

'I only took what I needed so that those whose livin' I support wouldn't suffer,' Holden Bauldry explained, playing the empathy card for all it was worth. 'If I could get the same from less land, I would gladly give some of it up. I am only doin' what anybody else would do if they were in my situation. After all, you ain't no saint, Comyn, stealin' my cattle!'

'I would steal land back from yer if I could, Bauldry, but it's easier to steal your cattle. Besides, I ain't the one on trial here. I had my trial last year an' I got off. Wonder if you will yours, but more of that later. Right now, I'm feelin' hungry an' thirsty, so I'm gonna adjourn this court for lunch. Mex, you go across the road to the store; see if they got any beans or rice, or somethin' we could cook up. Hobo, you go an' get that woman from upstairs an' watch over her while she cooks whatever Mex comes back with.'

Mack looked out of the window and watched as Mose scribbled on a sheet of paper, wrap it around a small stone and threw it up towards the window. Mack caught it first time; they were getting good at this.

'There's a wagon and bales of hay inside Meggan's livery,' he whispered to Della. 'I know what to do,' he muttered as he started scribbling a response.

'Someone's coming,' Della whispered. 'It's that leery Hobo.' Mack screwed the piece of paper he was writing on into a ball, threw it out of the window and hauled the curtain inside.

'Yer wanned downstairs, woman,' Hobo said gruffly as he laid down sufficient floorboards for her to walk out along the hall. 'We're hungry. You gotta cook us somethin' to eat!'

'Miss Peveril! Good day to you, ma'am,' Dean Comyn said sarcastically.

'I hear you're lookin' for someone to be subservient,' Della said in an equally sarcastic tone.

'Well, we'd like to have some food cooked an' I figured that you ain't got much to do right now,' Comyn replied with a smirk on his face. 'Hobo, take her to the kitchen. Mex, after lunch you need to go down to the corral, get some rope and rig up a noose. Bauldry don't know this yet, but he's about to eat his last supper. Oh, an' while you're down there, check on that slouch Trigger in the jail.' Della tried not to show any concern at the mention of Trigger's name but if Mex checked the jail he'd find that Mose had escaped. She knew that that could spell a quick end for all of them if Dean's patience was provoked and he decided to put an immediate stop to his courtroom drama and play-acting.

Della was equally shocked but not surprised at the state of the hotel kitchen. Broken windows meant that there was dust everywhere: in the pantry, over the crockery and cutlery and pots and pans. Mex had wiped the dust off a table with his sleeve and placed the ingredients for their food, which he had obtained from the store across the road, on its surface. Otherwise, there was no food in the storerooms. It had all gone: eaten by the rats, although without any ready source of food they had long vacated the hotel as well. The only sign of life were the plants growing through the gaps in the broken floorboards. From the recent biology lesson she had given before she came away, Della recognized one of the plants from its blue violet bloom as the camas lily. The only piece of equipment that eventually proved itself to have survived the long period of neglect was the stove.

'What food did Mex get?' Della asked. Hobo looked in the bags.

'Er . . . looks like salt pork, potatoes and cabbage,' Hobo replied.

'We're gonna need lots of booze to clean utensils and cook with,' Della pointed out. 'There's no clean water. Where's the cellar?'

'Over there,' said Hobo, pointing towards the far end of the kitchen. 'D'yer wan' me to go an' get it?'

'No. I know what I'm lookin' for. I'll get it,' Della replied.

'Bring me a bottle o' whiskey an' I'll see you alright, Miss Della,' Hobo said. She nodded, pushed the cellar door open and walked down the three wooden steps, leaving the cellar door ajar to create sufficient light. As she turned around she saw a figure emerge from behind the cellar door. Her heart froze.

'Oh, it's you, Mose,' she whispered regaining her breath. 'What are you doing here?'

'Actin' on Mack's last message. He wanted several cases of

spirits taken to the livery. I got in from the bar.'

'Listen,' Della said. 'I've gotta cook them lunch, but afterwards the one called Mex has been told to get some hanging rope and check on the jail. Can you do something?'

'Don't worry, Miss Della. I'll be gone,' Mose whispered.

Della decided to boil the potatoes in a large saucepan of white wine and fry the pork. Hobo watched her cook, as he swigged on the bottle of whiskey she had found him. While he was very aware of her presence, she was oblivious to his. He put his bottle down and sidled around behind her, putting his right arm around her waist.

'I don't know what smells nicer,' he said, pressing his cheek against hers, 'You or the cookin'.'

'Go away,' Della urged. 'You've had too much to drink.'

'I don't think so,' he said. 'Not yet. What's this?' He slid his hand deep into her left-hand dress pocket and his fingers fumbled around her thigh before returning to her waist. 'I thought so,' he whispered in her left ear. As Della struggled, Hobo tightened his grip around her waist.

'Very clever,' he said. 'You've fitted a small holster in the pocket of your dress, hangin' from an adjustable leather belt sewn into the waistband. So where's the Derringer that goes in that holster, eh?'

'I didn't bring it with me. It's at home,' Della lied.

'So why did you wear this dress but not bother to bring the gun?'

'It's one of my old dresses from when I was a showgirl. Girls in that profession often carry guns but I don't need to carry one anymore.'

'You sure it's not upstairs?' Hobo asked. 'I'd hate for Mr Comyn to find out about this.'

'I gave you a bottle of whiskey. You said you'd see me all right,' Della pleaded, sounding scared.

'It'll take more than that, little darlin',' Hobo muttered, leaving Della to get on with the cooking.

'Is that dinner ready yet?' Hobo asked. 'We're hungry.'

'I guess so,' Della replied. 'I was going to add some wild onions but most of 'em are still way too hard and would need to boil for a lot longer. There's a tray over there so you can take these dinners in. You'll have to come back for yours.'

'If any of 'em onions are a bit soft you can put 'em on my plate. I like onions,' Hobo said as he left the kitchen. Della bent down and, with an old apron she had found, pulled up a different camus onion plant carefully from the gaps in the damaged floorboards: one with a smaller, white flower. This camus plant had different properties from the blue flowered one. There was no time to cook the bulb so she removed the leaves, cut them up and applied them as a garnish to Hobo's dinner. He took his plate from her.

'I've put some onion garnish on yours,' she informed him.

'Good,' he replied. 'But we'll still need to come to an arrangement about the Derringer, Della,' Hobo pointed out.

'After lunch,' she proposed.

As Mose stared out of the cell window, he saw Mex in the corral taking a coil of rope from one of the horses. He'd propped the dead Trigger up in his chair, his head in his hand, hiding the bloodstain on his shirt and his hat pulled down over his face. The half bottle of whiskey on the desk in front of him would have automatically suggested to anyone looking in through the cell window from outside: drunk man, not dead man.

'Hey, kid,' Mex called out. 'If you were gonna hang a man

aroun' here, where would yer do it?'

'The old cotton wood tree immediately behind the well,' Mose answered, as he held his already cocked revolver below the window.

'Thanks, kid.' Mex strode over and looked in through the cell window. 'I see Trigger's sleepin' off the booze again. When he awakes tell 'im he missed a fine lunch! See ya.'

CHAPTER 22

'Afraid it's time for the rope, Bauldry,' Dean Comyn said as sympathetically as he could. 'Sorry it's taken so long, but you had a lot to say for yerself, although none of it was very convincing. OK, Mex, let's walk him slowly up the road. Hobo, you go upstairs and get Cambray an' the woman. Do 'em good to watch this, but we'll spare the kid from this next part of the ceremony. Leave him with Trigger.'

As his two colleagues left the hotel with their prisoner, Hobo staggered upstairs. He had never felt so ill in his life. As he wiped away the dribble from his mouth with the back of his hand, he noticed that it looked like froth. In spite of feeling that he was going to vomit at any moment, he managed to hold onto the banister and haul himself upstairs. Having forgotten about replacing the floorboards, he walked along the joists as he approached Della's room. Peering through the doorway, he thought he was going to black out. The room kept changing from light to dark but, regardless, there was no one there. Hobo rubbed his eyes and tried steadying himself on the joist but, as his body began convulsing, he lost his balance and fell to his death two floors below, a victim of poisoning from the death camus plant.

Holden Bauldry was frogmarched along Commercial Street towards the site of the well, opposite Meggan's livery, by Mex and Comyn. Dean had planned for Holden Bauldry to be hung in much the same way as Shorty: with his hands gripping the rope above his head, preventing the noose from being pulled tight around his neck until the strength in his arms gave out. They forced Holden to stand on the stone wall that surrounded the well, while Mex grabbed the noose that he had rigged up on the horizontal branch of the old cottonwood tree earlier and dropped it over Bauldry's neck.

'I can't see Hobo comin', boss,' Mex said, looking back down the street. 'Shall I go and look for 'im?'

Dean Comyn quickly weighed up the prospect in his mind that maybe Hobo had been jumped by his prisoners in an attempt to save Bauldry from the hangman's noose. 'No, we hang Bauldry immediately. Push him off the wall!' Comyn shouted, feeling a little uneasy. No sooner had he spoke than the double doors of the livery were flung open, and a wagon full of freshly lit straw was pushed across the street and stopped in front of Dean Comyn, blocking his view of the well. As Mose Alder jumped up onto the well wall, he grabbed hold of Mex and pulled him backwards. The rustler let out a bloodcurdling scream as he fell down the well, fracturing his skull against its stone lining before landing in a dead, huddled heap at the bottom.

Mack Cambray ran around the well and took a flying leap at the horizontal branch of the old cottonwood tree. As he suspected, the branch was rotten. The tree had died as the well had dried up and the water table dropped. The loud cracking sound of the breaking branch was the cue for Holden Bauldry to remove the noose from around his neck as the branch crashed to the ground.

'What the hell's goin' on?' screamed Dean Comyn as the bottles of spirit concealed in the burning straw began exploding in the flames, showering shards of molten glass over him. With the intense heat in front of him and the wooden wall of the building behind him, Comyn was left with only two choices of escape. He could either head south, across the open corral and risk being shot down, or cross over Commercial Street to the relative safety of the buildings on its north side. He chose the latter but, as he headed for Meggan's livery, he came under rifle fire from the top floor of the two-storey building. He looked up; it was Della Peveril. Running, he fired off a couple of rounds with his revolver. He aimed to miss. If he could capture Della Peveril, she would be his bargaining chip to safety. Aware of her vulnerability, Della fired one last shot before Comyn disappeared from view and began to climb the outside stairs. Nursing his trigger hand, which had been winged by Della's bullet, Dean Comyn dropped his gun down the stairs. With Mack Cambray making his way across the street, there was no time to go back and pick it up. Comyn continued to mount the stairs.

Unable to load the next bullet, Della flung the jammed rifle down on the floor. She was in trouble. She reached in her dress pocket for her Derringer. She had never fired it in anger before. It had just two bullets, an accuracy range of a few yards and, although not guaranteed to down someone permanently, it could kill if fired at very close quarters. Comyn burst through the door, brandishing his remaining weapons: his anger and the knife he had taken from his boot.

'Shoot, Della, shoot!' Mack Cambray's voice boomed from the bottom of the stairs. She pulled the trigger. There was a loud bang, but still Dean Comyn came towards her. One bullet left; one last attempt before he would be on her. She fired again. Comyn staggered. She saw the blood on his face. He hovered momentarily, as if suspended in time, before falling dead at her feet.

EPILOGUE

'Goodbye, Holden,' Della said, shaking his hand. 'Mack's travelling back with me to keep me company and keep me safe. Thanks for everything; it all worked out OK in the end. Your nephew was a hero.'

'Yes,' Holden replied. 'He sure was. He really came through this time. Always knew he had it in him. Good luck to you, Della. And Mack,' he said, turning towards Mack Cambray, 'I guess I'll see you in a week's time. I'm ready for you to search my land for water so that I can give some of my acres back to the community. To think for a long time I thought of you as just another line rider down on his luck, but clearly you are so much more than that.'

'Thanks, Holden,' Mack replied, shaking the cattleman's hand. 'I think we've probably surprised each other as to what we're both really made of. See you next week.'